The Robot Needs Eyes

Warily, Johnny looked around: he was in a room with rough stone walls and he was lying on a table. Near him, on a marble-topped washstand, glittering instruments—a scalpel, a probe—lay in a row. At the far end of the room stood something large—a statue, maybe—that was draped with a painter's drop cloth.

"So here we are. Isn't this a nice place?" the old man crooned. "Now before we begin, I wonder if you'd care to see my new creation. Alas, this will be your only chance to see it, so make the most of your opportunity."

Johnny heard footsteps moving down to the other end of the room. There was a swishing sound, then the footsteps returned. The old man propped Johnny's head up and he saw the thing that had been hidden by the drop cloth. His heart began to hammer hard. There on a stone pedestal stood a gaunt figure made of shining metal. The head was like a skull covered with glittering skin, and the large hollow eye sockets were empty. . . .

THE EYES
OF THE
KILLER ROBOT

❦

JOHN BELLAIRS

Frontispiece
by Edward Gorey

A BANTAM SKYLARK BOOK®
NEW YORK · TORONTO · LONDON · SYDNEY · AUCKLAND

RL 6, 009–013

*This low-priced Bantam Book
has been completely reset in a typeface
designed for easy reading, and was printed
from new plates. It contains the complete
text of the original hardcover edition.*
NOT ONE WORD HAS BEEN OMITTED.

THE EYES OF THE KILLER ROBOT

*A Bantam Book / published by arrangement with
Dial Press*

PRINTING HISTORY

Dial Press edition published October 1986

*Skylark Books is a registered trademark of Bantam Books, Inc.
Registered in U.S. Patent and Trademark Office and elsewhere.*

Cover art by Edward Gorey

Bantam Skylark edition / December 1987

ISBN 0-553-15552-0

Published simultaneously in the United States and Canada

*Bantam Books are published by Bantam Books, Inc. Its trademark, consisting of
the words "Bantam Books" and the portrayal of a rooster, is Registered in U.S. Patent
and Trademark Office and in other countries. Marca Registrada. Bantam Books, Inc.,
666 Fifth Avenue, New York, New York 10103.*

PRINTED IN THE UNITED STATES OF AMERICA

0 9 8 7 6

The Eyes of
the Killer Robot

CHAPTER ONE

⚬═⚬

"Go foul, you dirty dog! Go foul!"

Professor Childermass was on his feet, yelling and waving his arm toward the right field foul line. In his left hand he held a hot dog, and it was dripping mustard on his shoe. As the professor watched, the long fly ball twisted foul into the stands. With a relieved sigh, he sat down and took a bite of his hot dog. *"Okay, Bullard!"* he roared. *"That's two strikes, and you know what comes next, you big stupid clodhopper!"*

It was a summer day in the early nineteen-fifties, and Professor Roderick Childermass was at Boston's Fenway Park with his young friend Johnny Dixon. They were watching a baseball game between the Red Sox and the Yankees, and they were having a great time—except that

Johnny got embarrassed sometimes, when the professor started screeching and yelling. They were an odd pair: the professor was short and elderly and crabby-looking, with wildly sprouting muttonchop whiskers, gold-rimmed glasses, and a nose that looked like an overripe strawberry. Johnny also wore glasses, but he was pale and blond-haired, and about thirteen years old. Strange as it may seem, these two were good friends: Johnny lived with his grandfather and grandmother in the town of Duston Heights, Massachusetts, and the professor lived across the street. Although he had a rotten temper, the professor was a very kind and thoughtful person, and he had become sort of a foster father to Johnny. He took him places and baked cakes for him and listened to the things that he had to say. Johnny was shy and brainy and he did not make friends easily: except for the professor, he had only one other good friend in the world, a smart-alecky kid named Fergie Ferguson. A lot of people wondered why Johnny hung around with a cranky old man who was in his mid-seventies, but Johnny never wondered—he knew that his life would be a lot poorer and a lot emptier without the old man.

However, there were times when Johnny wished that he was far, far away from the professor. He was a quiet kid, so he always got upset when his elderly friend ranted and raved loudly at baseball games. Right now the professor was razzing one of the Yankee heavy hitters, the big left fielder, Cliff Bullard. He was up with two men on and two out in the eighth inning, and his team was behind.

Bullard was not a nice guy: he was tough and egotistical and swaggering and mean. Also he was in a batting slump, and that did not help his mood any. As Bullard stood watching, the Red Sox manager went out to talk to his pitcher, and the professor went on yelling. The seats that he and Johnny were sitting in were close to the first-base line, so Bullard could hear every word. His face was getting red, and now and then he would glance angrily at the little old man who was giving him such a hard time.

"Please, professor!" said Johnny timidly. "I don't think you ought to yell so loud! That guy might get mad and come over here!"

The professor chuckled nastily. "Don't worry!" he said. "The big ape wouldn't dare show that he's upset— these Boston fans would climb all over him if he popped off at me. Relax! Razzing and bench-jockeying are part of the Great American Pastime. *Hey, Bullard! Is it true you have sawdust where your brain is supposed to be?*"

The Boston manager walked back to the dugout, and the pitcher went into the stretch. He reared back and let fly with a blazing fastball, and Bullard swung so hard that he almost fell down. The umpire yelled "*Strrrike three!*" and jerked his thumb in the air. After throwing another hateful look at the professor, Bullard turned and stalked back to the dugout with his bat in his hand. The Boston players trotted off the field, the crowd roared, and the professor started to laugh.

"I *love* to see that sort of thing happen!" he chortled. "Did you see the look he gave me? Oooh, was he mad!"

Johnny said nothing, but he winced slightly. He did not like the look that Bullard had given the professor, he did not like it at all. But then he told himself not to be such a nervous nit, and he went back to enjoying the game. The bottom of the eighth inning and the top of the ninth passed, and the Red Sox won. The professor and Johnny joined the crowd that was streaming out of the exits and into the street. As they walked, the professor began telling stories about old-time baseball players, like Van Lingle Mungo and Nap Lajoie. Suddenly he stopped. A large poster on a wall outside the ball park caught his eye. It was very colorful, with red and blue lettering and little hands pointing to important parts. The sign said:

BIG STRIKEOUT CONTEST!

During the week of October 12th to the 18th, Yankee slugger CLIFF BULLARD will be visiting stadiums and ball parks all over the state of Massachusetts. He challenges all local pitchers to try to strike him out! Believing that it will be impossible for anyone to do this, Mr. Bullard offers TEN THOUSAND SILVER DOLLARS as a prize. Strike him out, and the dollars are YOURS! CAN IT BE DONE? Come and find out, baseball fans!

With folded arms, the professor glared at the poster. "Humph!" he snorted. "If that isn't just like him! Cliff Bullard, world's greatest baseball player! Boy, wouldn't I love to see somebody throw three quick strikes past the big plug-ugly. Would *he* ever be surprised!" The professor sighed, and with a shrug of his shoulders, he turned away. "However," he added, "it isn't very likely that a local kid from Lynn or Marblehead would be able to do the trick. I mean, Cliff Bullard is a dangerous hitter—he's a creep, but he's murder with a bat in his hands. Big league pitchers can handle him—sometimes—but your average high school or college hurler couldn't. No, the money he's offering is pretty safe. He'll never have to . . ."

The professor's voice trailed away, and a strange look came into his eyes. He rubbed his chin and grinned and made odd murmuring noises.

Johnny stared at the old man. "Professor, what's wrong? What're you thinking about?"

"Hm?" said the professor. He smiled vaguely and then shook his head, as if he were trying to wake himself up. "Oh—oh, yes. Well, if you must know, I was just remembering something that happened a long time ago. It was an odd incident, and your grampa was involved. But instead of telling you about it now, why don't we drive to the place where it all happened, and then I'll tell you. It's not very far from home. Come on."

The drive back to Duston Heights took about two hours, and the sun was low in the sky when they got there. But instead of driving into town, the professor swerved onto a side road. They drove past country stores and fire stations until they came to a weedy overgrown field with an old sagging green grandstand in the middle of it. The car rolled to a halt on the sandy shoulder next to the road, and the professor turned the motor off. Johnny got out and followed the professor over a rusty wire fence. As they got closer to the grandstand, Johnny could see that this was an abandoned baseball diamond. There was the pitcher's mound, and the lines of the basepaths could still be seen. Over all this the gaunt, wrecked grandstand loomed: its roof was full of holes, and the seats were warped and split and rotten.

Johnny looked around in awe. It was like visiting some ancient Roman ruin. "Who used to play here, professor?" he asked. "Was it a team from Duston Heights?"

The professor nodded. "Yes, it was. It was a semiprofessional team called the Spiders, and they were pretty darned good. Your grampa played for them back around 1900. Did you know that?"

Johnny's jaw dropped. "Really? He never told me that!"

The professor smiled sadly. "No, he wouldn't have— Henry's not the sort who would brag about his past accomplishments. But in his day your grampa was known as Cyclone Dixon. He had a blazing fastball, and his curveball wasn't so bad either. He won lots of games, but his career ended when a batter hit a line drive that smashed his big toe. He tried to come back and play before the toe was completely healed, and he changed his pitching style. After that he was never any good. But that's not what I brought you out here to talk about. I wanted to tell you about something very strange that happened in this ball park in the summer of 1901."

"What was it?" asked Johnny, who was really beginning to get interested.

The professor smiled mysteriously. "Come over here and sit down, and I'll tell you."

Johnny followed the professor over to the grandstands, and they sat down on one of the lower seats. The professor fumbled in his jacket pocket for cigarettes, lit one, and began to talk about a crazy inventor named Evaristus Sloane. Sloane had lived in a little town up in New Hampshire, but he came down to Duston Heights now and then to sell—or try to sell—his inventions. Actually, Sloane made his living as a blacksmith, but in his spare time he invented things—odd contraptions that nobody needed, like an eight-man tandem bicycle, and coffins equipped with whistles and bells that you could use if you got buried alive. All of Sloane's inventions flopped, and he got kind of bitter about it, but one bright summer day he came out to the ball park with a brand-new gadget: a pitching machine.

"You mean one of those catapult things that serve balls up to the plate so batters can practice their hitting?" asked Johnny.

The professor nodded. "Sort of. The odd thing about this machine was, it was shaped like a man. A big metal man with a metal baseball cap, a metal uniform, and a cast-iron arm that could heave a baseball at speeds up to one hundred and ten miles an hour." The professor sighed and puffed at his cigarette. "Now, you would think," he went on, "that this would be just the kind of machine that baseball players would want. They could use it for batting practice, and there would be no danger that one of their good pitchers might get hurt. At first, a lot of the players on the Spiders' team thought that Sloane's robot would be a great thing for them to have, but in the end they decided not to buy it."

Johnny blinked. "Why not?"

The professor smiled oddly. "Why not? Because your grandfather didn't like the blamed thing. He said there was something uncanny about it, something evil. For one thing, he didn't like the way the robot stared at him. He didn't like its eyes."

"Its *eyes*?"

The professor nodded. "Mm-hmm. That's what I said: its eyes. The robot had big staring glass eyes, and your grampa said that they really gave him the willies. Weird, eh? Well, your grampa talked to the other players, and he argued a bit. Finally he threatened to leave the team if they bought Sloane's robot." The professor rolled his eyes upward and grimaced. "As you might imagine," he went on, "that really did it! The Spiders did not want to lose a star player like Cyclone Dixon, and so they told Evaristus Sloane to get lost."

"What did Sloane do?" asked Johnny. "Did he get mad?"

The professor laughed. "Mad? He was *furious*! He told everybody off, and he said some very unpleasant things to your grandfather. Then he got some of the players to help him put the robot back into his wagon, and he drove off, still cursing and swearing. But that's not the end of the story."

Johnny looked puzzled. "It isn't?"

"Nope," said the professor. "It definitely is not. You see, a few weeks later, the great hitter 'Clutch' Klemm showed up in town—he was playing for another semipro team, the Pittsfield Turtles. Well, in his day, Klemm was as famous as our boy Bullard, and he arranged a contest just like the one we saw advertised on that poster at Fenway Park. Klemm offered one hundred dollars to anyone who could strike him out. Well, in those days, a hundred bucks was a lot of money, so all the Spiders' pitchers tried their best, but it was no use: Klemm lambasted the ball everywhere, and he even hit one shot that was longer than any that had ever been hit out of this ball park. Your grampa tried like everyone else, but he failed too. Well, at this point the sky started to get dark, as if there was a storm coming on, and out from behind the grandstand walked a man no one had ever seen before. He was tall and big-boned and he walked rather stiffly, and he had big, staring blue eyes. He walked right up to the managers of the two teams and asked if he could have a crack at winning the hundred dollars. Everybody was kind of startled, but they figured, heck, let the guy try, and Klemm picked up a bat. The strange guy trotted out to the mound then, and he went into his windup and threw."

Johnny edged forward on his seat. "So what happened then?"

The professor smiled. "What happened? Why, the first pitch came in so fast that Klemm couldn't see it. He swung at the second one, but he was way too late. And the third one was a cannon shot that darned near knocked the catcher down. Klemm swung at where he thought the ball was, but he was way too late. So the big lug won the contest, and he collected his hundred bucks, and he just walked away over the fields and vanished. No one ever saw him again. And now I'll tell you something very strange, John: Several of the people who watched the strange man pitch claimed that he was Sloane's robot!"

Johnny was startled. "The *robot*! How the heck could that be possible, professor?"

The professor shrugged. "You've got me. All I'm telling you is what people said after the strikeout contest was over. Folks sometimes get peculiar ideas into their heads—though I will have to admit that this idea was more peculiar than most. How could a living man be a robot, or vice versa? Even if Sloane had dressed his robot up in street clothes . . . well, even then, the figure was mounted on a little platform that rolled along on iron wheels, and it had a shiny metal face. No, it would never be mistaken for a living, breathing human being, unless . . . unless . . ."

Johnny leaned forward eagerly. "Yeah? Unless what, professor?"

The professor sighed and shook his head. "Unless nothing, John. As usual, I don't know what I'm talking about. Look, my rear end is getting cold from sitting on this bench, and besides, I promised your grandmother that I'd try to get you home before dark. Let's get a move on."

The professor got up, stretched, and started walking toward the car. Johnny followed, but as he went he turned and looked at the grassy hump that had once been the pitcher's mound. His grandfather had been out there pitching once upon a time. It was strange to think about. The story of the Man from Nowhere was also pretty strange, and it really fascinated Johnny. What did the professor mean by saying *unless* at the end of his tale? Was he just being silly, or was there really some way that a robot could pose as a human being? Johnny thought about this problem for a long time—as they rode on home, and while he ate his late supper, and as he lay in bed that night, waiting for sleep to come. But he didn't come up with any answers.

CHAPTER TWO

❦

The next morning, Johnny decided that he would ask Grampa about Evaristus Sloane and his robot. Grampa Dixon was a tall, slightly stooped old man with a high, domed forehead and a saggy, friendly face. He was standing at the kitchen stove pouring a cup of coffee when Johnny popped his question.

"The . . . the professor was telling me about old Evaristus Sloane yesterday," said Johnny, hesitantly. "Is it all true? I mean, about the robot with the glass eyes?"

Grampa Dixon set the coffeepot down and turned around slowly. The look in his eyes showed that he was surprised and a bit upset. "My gosh!" he said. "What the heck got into Rod, anyway? Why'd he drag that old story outa the closet?"

"It's true, then, isn't it?" said Johnny excitedly. Then he added uncertainly, "I mean, did it really happen?"

Grampa nodded and sipped his coffee. "Oh, yeah, it's true all right!" he muttered. "Only . . . well, I don't like t'think about Sloane very much. He must be dead by now, but I still can't get him outa my mind. He was a bad one, a real rotten egg, an' I still remember what he said to me that day, when I made the ball club turn him an' his robot down."

Johnny was extremely curious now. "Why, Grampa? What did he say?"

Grampa's mouth curled into a grim frown. "He said he'd get even with me, if it was the last thing he did. I dunno why, but I really took him seriously. I mean, what he said scared me, an' I had bad dreams about him later."

Johnny stared. "Did . . . did anything bad ever happen to you later?" he asked. "Did Sloane ever come to your house and try to—"

Grampa cut him off with a shake of his head. "Nope. He never did nothin' to me. But the trouble is, I still think about him every so often, an' I really wish Rod hadn't told you about him. Now, if y' don't mind, I got t'go out an' cut the grass. See ya later, Johnny."

And with that, Grampa set his coffee cup down on the kitchen table and left the room. With a bewildered look on his face, Johnny watched him go. He had figured that Grampa would be amused by the old story, and maybe even proud of the part he had played in it. Instead he seemed to be irritated and frightened. But what was there to be scared of? Evaristus Sloane was dead, and the incident with the robot had happened over fifty years ago. Johnny thought about Grampa's strange reaction as he munched his cornflakes. Maybe he should run upstairs and ask Gramma, who was making the beds and dusting the bedroom furniture. She always enjoyed gossiping about the old days, and she might know something about Sloane. But for some reason, Johnny didn't want to find out what Gramma knew. He was getting a little scared himself, and he decided that maybe he'd better let the whole thing drop.

A few days later, Johnny and his friend Fergie were out hiking, not far from Duston Heights. Fergie was a gangly, droopy-faced kid with big ears and a long, blunt-ended nose. He was a smart-alecky, wisecracking type, and he was the only kid Johnny really enjoyed hanging around with. The two of them had met one year at Boy Scout camp, and they had gotten to be good friends. Now that it was summer, and school was out, Fergie and Johnny spent a lot of time going on long walks together. On this particular day they were swinging along on a dusty gravel road that wound past cornfields and farmhouses. As they walked, they sang marching songs and told jokes and tried to stump each other with questions about weird historical facts. They rounded a corner and started down a hill, and Johnny happened to glance to his left. What he saw made him stop suddenly—there, not far away, stood the old half-ruined grandstand that he had visited not long ago, when the professor first told him the story of Evaristus Sloane and his robot.

"Hey!" Johnny exclaimed as he reached out and grabbed Fergie's arm. "Hey, Fergie! Over there!"

Fergie looked, and he smiled sourly. Johnny had told him the professor's story, and Fergie had not believed one word of it. Fergie was a pretty skeptical kid, and he was always making fun of Johnny for being gullible. "Yeah, I see it," he muttered in a bored voice. "I've seen the place before—I live around here, remember? An' I have heard everything that I want to hear about the guy with the electric whizmagiggy, or whatever it was. C'mon, I'll race you to the bottom o' this hill."

"Can't we just go over there and poke around for a minute?" asked Johnny plaintively. "It'd only take a minute or two."

Fergie gave Johnny an irritated glance, but then he grinned and shrugged. "Oh, well, why not?" he said carelessly. "We haven't got anything better to do. Let's go."

The two of them left the road, plodded up a short steep bank, and clambered over a sagging wire fence. As they tramped across the dry stubble, clouds of midges hovered about them. The long level rays of the setting sun fell on the splintered wood of the old grandstand and the weedy overgrown baseball diamond. It occurred to Johnny that this was the same time of day that it had been when he and the professor had been here. *Maybe I was meant to come here again,* he thought. This was a weird idea, and he would never have spoken it out loud. But he believed in things that were "meant to be," no matter how hard he tried not to.

For a while Johnny and Fergie just fooled around. Fergie had a small rubber ball in his pocket, and Johnny found a fairly straight branch in a pile of dry brush by the roadside, so they were able to play stickball. But Johnny had trouble seeing the ball in the fading light, and after a little while they just went over to the grandstand, sat down, and drank from the canteen of water they had brought with them. In the hollow space under the sagging roof, shadows were gathering. The sun was gone now, and a faint orange afterglow hung in the sky. Johnny fell into a thoughtful mood. He had the odd feeling that something was going to happen, though he didn't have any idea of what it might be. Suddenly he was startled by a sound that seemed to come from inside the grandstand.

"Huh?" he said, glancing quickly over his shoulder. "Did you hear that? What was it?"

Fergie snickered. "It was the mullygrubs. They're comin' to carry us off an' turn us into Baby Ruth candy bars. What a horrible fate for two innocent youngsters like us."

Johnny gave Fergie a dirty look. "You think I'm just a nervous nit, don't you?" he grumbled.

"Yeah, I do," said Fergie cheerfully as he scrambled to his feet. "Tell ya what, John baby. I'm gonna run down to that bent-over tree an' back an' you can time me with your watch. Then we're gonna have to hit the road; it's gettin' dark. Ready? Here I go!"

Johnny opened his mouth to say that he couldn't read his watch face in the darkness under the grandstand roof.

But it was no use: Fergie was off like a cannon shot, elbows and knees pumping madly. With a sigh, Johnny sank back into his seat. He sat very still watching his friend run, and then a strange feeling began to steal over him. He felt cold and alone, as if he were the last person left on the face of the earth. Gripping his knees hard with his hands, he stared rigidly ahead, and then he heard a voice behind him. A hollow disembodied voice that said, *"They took my eyes. . . . They took my eyes."*

When Fergie got back, puffing and panting, he found Johnny sitting perfectly still. "Hey, John baby, how'd I do?" he gasped. "Break any records, did I?"

No response. Johnny sat stiff as a statue, and suddenly it dawned on Fergie that Johnny was scared half out of his mind. For once Fergie did not feel like kidding. He stood silent for a second, and then he reached down and gently tapped Johnny on the shoulder.

"Hey, John," he said softly. "Are . . . are you okay?"

Johnny swallowed hard, but he still didn't move. When he spoke, his lips just barely fluttered. "There's something up in the dark behind me. I heard it. We gotta get out of here." Johnny's voice was lifeless and flat, like a recording.

Now it was Fergie's turn to be scared. He had heard of people who went crazy all of a sudden, for no reason. On the other hand, there might really be something to be scared of. Fergie peered up into the well of darkness that hung over their heads. If there was some smart-aleck kid or some old bum hiding up there, Byron Q. Ferguson could handle him.

"You stay here a minute," he said quietly as he gave Johnny another reassuring pat on the shoulder. "I'll be back in a minute."

Fergie started climbing. A little light seeped in through chinks and cracks in the back of the grandstand, so it was not quite as dark as it had seemed at first. Nimbly he vaulted up over the rows of split and sagging seats, and as he went he turned his head from side to side, squinting into the moldy-smelling gloom. But he saw no one, no one at all. When he had almost reached the top of the stands, his hand struck something small and hard that was sitting on one of the benches. It flew off onto the wooden floor with a tiny clink and clatter. Quickly Fergie reached down and picked up the object: it was a small, oval box made of metal. With a puzzled frown, he stuffed the box into his pants pocket. Then he turned and began picking his way back down to the place where Johnny was sitting. When he got to the bottom, Fergie was glad to see Johnny standing there and peering up at him—at least he wasn't paralyzed any more.

"Hi, Fergie," said Johnny weakly. He felt ashamed, like someone who has been caught doing something cowardly. "I . . . I'm sorry I got so scared, but I heard this voice and—hey, did you see anybody?"

Fergie shook his head. "Nope. But I found this." He reached into his pocket and pulled out the small, oval box. "Here," he said as he handed it to Johnny. "Do you know what the heck this is?"

Johnny took the box from Fergie and turned it over in his hands. Motioning for Fergie to follow him, he walked out to the center of the baseball field, where some dim light still lingered. Now he could see that there was an enameled picture on the hinged lid of the box: it showed a beggar with a staff picking his way along a country road. Tilting the lid up, Johnny reached inside the box and pulled out a folded scrap of paper. As he opened it, Fergie crowded in to have a look. At the top of the paper the number 896 was scrawled in ink, and below it a name was stamped in ornate Victorian letters: CHIGWELL'S PAWN SHOP.

"What the devil . . ." said Fergie quietly. At first Johnny said nothing. He threw a nervous glance over his shoulder at the dark grandstand, and then he closed his fist tight around the little box.

"We'd better go show this to the professor," he said. "He knows all about old-fashioned things, and maybe he can help us."

Later that evening, the professor sat at his kitchen table and peered owlishly at the box. Nearby on the scarred white tabletop lay the piece of paper, and behind the professor stood Johnny and Fergie. Their arms were folded, and they both looked puzzled.

"Well, to end your suspense, gentlemen, this is a snuff-box," said the professor, and he set the thing down with a loud rap. "Eighteenth-century gentlemen used to carry them around, though I'm not sure this one is really that old. As for the paper, it is a very old pawn ticket. You know how these things work, don't you? Somebody goes into a pawn shop and gives the man a guitar or a gold watch or something and gets money for it. With the money you get a pawn ticket, and that allows you to buy back the object that you pawned within sixty days or whatever length of time is decided on by the pawnbroker. But all this is beside the point. What I want to know is this: What were this box and this note doing on a seat in that old ruined grandstand? And that voice you heard, John. What was it that the voice said?"

Johnny looked solemn. "It said *They took my eyes.* The voice said it twice, and that was all."

The professor twisted around in his chair and glared up at Johnny. "Was it a man's voice or a woman's?"

Johnny hesitated. "A—a man's, I think. It was kind of hollow and whispery, but it sounded like a man. We didn't see anyone though—did we, Fergie?"

Fergie shook his head. "Nope, we sure didn't."

"Humph!" said the professor, and he wrinkled up his nose in a discontented way. For a long while he was silent. He seemed to be thinking, and he kept turning the snuffbox over and over in his hands. "Well!" he said, at last. "This is all very mysterious, not to mention strange, odd, and peculiar. It might interest you to know, by the way, that Chigwell's Pawn Shop is still in existence. It's down by that old row of leather-working shops on Washington Street—has either of you noticed it?"

"Yeah," Fergie put in. "I know where it is. My Uncle Howie pawned the family silverware there once, when he was outa work."

The professor grinned. "How interesting! Now then, gentlemen, what I think we ought to do is this: We should try to use this antiquated ticket to locate the object that was pawned long ago. I realize that there's not much chance of our coming up with anything, but you never know. Would you two like to go down to Chigwell's with me tomorrow morning?"

CHAPTER THREE

‿◉‿

Fergie and Johnny said yes enthusiastically. Around ten thirty the next morning, the two boys and the professor were standing outside of Chigwell's Pawn Shop. Three golden globes hung from a bracket over the door, and propped up behind the plate-glass display window were two guitars, a saxophone, a velvet-covered board with several antique watches hanging on it, and an old cavalry saber. There was also an enormous meerschaum pipe covered with carved satyrs and nymphs, and a brass-lined wastebasket made from the foot of a rhinoceros. After the three of them had studied the things in the window for a few minutes, the professor coughed loudly and said, "Come along, gentlemen! Time's awasting!" He went into the shop, and Fergie and Johnny followed him.

The owner of the shop was a small, bald, meek-looking man who wore half-moon glasses and an unbuttoned gray vest. The professor marched straight up to the man, introduced himself, and fished the pawn ticket out of his pocket. When the man saw the ticket, his eyes opened wide.

"Good night!" he exclaimed as he took the piece of paper from the professor's hand. "I never expected to see one of *these* again! Where on earth did you get it?"

The professor smiled uncomfortably and glanced away. "It's a long story—I won't bore you with it. To tell the truth, I'm amazed that you recognize the ticket. I know it seems unlikely, but I wonder if it's possible that you still have the object that the ticket belongs to."

The pawnbroker stared hard at the ticket and scratched the side of his nose. "Hmm . . ." he muttered. "You know, there is just an outside chance that we might have it. You see, this ticket comes from my grandfather's time, and a few years ago we gave away or sold a lot of stuff left over from the old days. But I saved a few rather curious objects that I just couldn't bear to get rid of. They're in a closet in the back room. Here. Let me go have a look."

The pawnbroker took the ticket and disappeared through a curtained doorway. A few minutes later he came back with an old-fashioned walking stick in his hands. The body of the cane was made of some mottled light-brown wood, and it was capped at the bottom by a tarnished brass ferrule. For a handle the cane had a piece of ivory that was shaped like a long, skinny human hand,

and the fingers of the hand clutched an ivory ball. Attached to the handle was an old tattered cardboard tag with the number 896 on it.

"Good grief!" exclaimed the professor. "So *that's* our prize, eh? Well, well!"

"That's it," said the man with a little sigh. He laid the cane on the counter, turned, and plucked a dust rag down from a shelf. As Fergie and Johnny crowded in to stare at the cane, the man began wiping the dust off it. "It's been in that closet back there ever since I can remember," he said. "When I was a kid playing in the back of this shop, I used to take it out and fool around with it, but I always made sure my dad didn't know what I was doing. It's a dangerous thing, you see."

The professor stared at him blankly. "Dangerous? How do you mean?"

The pawnbroker smiled and gripped the ivory handle firmly. He tugged, and out came a thin, springy sword blade.

"Wow!" exclaimed Fergie delightedly. "I've always wanted to have one of those! Can I see it?"

The man handed the sword to Fergie, and he turned it back and forth in the light. Running the whole length of the blade, on both sides, were fancy engraved decorations —whorls and squiggles and loops—that looked like complicated Boy Scout knots. Fergie tested the edge of the blade with his finger: it was razor-sharp.

"Boy!" said Fergie, grinning wickedly. "You could sure use this to get a seat on the bus, couldn't you?"

The professor winced. "Yes, I suppose you could, Byron," he said. "And you could also use it to get yourself a seat in the county jail. Carrying a concealed weapon is against the law, and that sword cane qualifies as a concealed weapon. Rich gentlemen used to carry them in the old days, when there were no street lights and thugs lurked in every alley." He turned to the pawnbroker and reached into his hip pocket for his wallet. "How much do you want for the thing, eh?"

The pawnbroker shrugged and smiled. "Take it—it's yours. People always think that pawnbrokers are greedy, so I like to prove them wrong sometimes. Anyway, since you found the ticket, I'd say the cane was meant to be yours. Wouldn't you agree?"

The professor was surprised and pleased, and he insisted on giving the man a ten dollar bill. Then he turned to Fergie, who was still fiddling with the sword. "Young Byron is really the one who found the ticket," he said, "and so by rights he ought to have the cane. Doesn't that seem reasonable to you, John?"

Johnny nodded. "Sure. I think Fergie ought to have it."

Fergie grinned appreciatively, but then he seemed to have second thoughts. He frowned and shook his head. "Nah, prof, you oughta take it," he said thoughtfully. "My mom is always worried that I'll turn into a juvenile delinquent, and if she finds out I have a toad sticker like this, she'll think I'm gonna be gettin' a zip gun next. Thanks, but no thanks."

The professor sighed and accepted the gift. After the

pawnbroker had wrapped the cane in brown paper and tied it with string, the professor tucked it under his arm, and the three of them left the shop. As they were walking down the street to the professor's car, a battered blue Ford came cruising slowly past. It went round the traffic circle in front of the post office and then came rolling back past the professor's maroon Pontiac. The professor, Johnny, and Fergie were standing by the car discussing the parking ticket that the professor had gotten while they were in the pawn shop. They didn't notice the Ford as it passed them a second time. It rolled down Washington Street, and then turned right onto a bumpy potholed alley that ran between two abandoned factories. The car halted, and the two people inside glanced around to see if anyone was watching them. But the alley was totally empty.

"Are you sure that's the Dixon boy?" asked the driver. She was a burly, bossy-looking old woman with bunchy gray hair, and she wore a white uniform, the kind that nurses in hospitals wear, and steel-rimmed spectacles. Her eyes were hard.

"Yes. That's the little snot, that's him for sure!" said her passenger, a tall old man with a mop of white hair. The skin of the man's face was loose and saggy, and near the end of his long, pointed nose was a wart the size of a pea. The man's eyes were watery and red-rimmed, and sometimes he would glare fiercely this way and that for no reason at all. "It's certainly him—no doubt about it!" the man went on in a clipped voice that sounded vaguely British. "I wish we were ready to take him now, but my project's just not finished. These old hands of mine won't obey their master the way they used to. You don't hold it against me that I'm working so slowly, do you?"

The woman glanced contemptuously at the man, and she seemed to be on the point of saying something nasty. But she forced her mouth into a cold smile. "No, my dearest. I don't mind. If the final result is going to be good, you ought to take all the time that you need. But tell me: Is that little cranky-looking old man the boy's grandfather?"

The man shook his head. "No. Henry Dixon is about as tall as I am. I saw him the other day watering his lawn, and I recognized him immediately." Suddenly the man seemed to be a seized with fierce anger. He clenched his long pale hands on his knees and ground his teeth. "I wish I had him here in this alley," he muttered bitterly. "I'd wring his neck and leave him for dogs to mangle! I hate him! I hate him now more than I did all those years ago. Filthy rotten lying dirt-eating—"

"Now, now . . ." said the woman soothingly. "You mustn't allow yourself to get too angry. Remember what that doctor told you about your heart! You needn't worry, you'll get your revenge in due time. Meanwhile, I think we might as well go back to my place, and I'll fix us some lunch. Then I'll drive you back up north and you can get to work on our little project again. I'll keep an eye on young Mr. Dixon until we're ready to use him."

The old man said nothing. His face was still red and twisted with rage, and he went on clawing at his knees.

After a quick glance at him, the woman shrugged and started the car.

Time passed. It was the middle of July, and the days were blazing hot. Fergie and Johnny played chess and drank iced tea by the gallon, and they went to movies and gobbled hot fudge sundaes at Peter's Sweet Shop. Sometimes, when they were sitting on the Dixons' front porch on a warm evening, they talked about the snuffbox and the sword cane. Both these things had come to them in a very mysterious way, and they wanted to know who the owner had been. The professor had gone over the box and the cane with a magnifying glass, but he did not find any initials or other identifying marks. He had also called up Mr. Chigwell, but he had not been any help either. He explained that his grandfather had never kept any record of the names of people who pawned things at his shop. The professor remarked that the owner had probably been a man, because snuffboxes and canes were carried around by men in the old days. But beyond that, they knew absolutely nothing.

As the month wore on, Johnny began to get the odd feeling that he was being watched. Every now and then he would be walking up Fillmore Street, and an old blue Ford would come cruising past. Johnny knew that there was more than one blue Ford in the world, but this one had a dented right fender and a missing hubcap. He had seen it downtown on Merrimack Street and in other places. It always seemed to be disappearing around a corner as he turned to look. Johnny knew that he sometimes imagined things, and at first he told himself that he was being silly. But then other odd things began to happen: the phone would ring late at night, and when Johnny got up and ran downstairs to answer it, he would hear nothing but a dial tone at the other end. And twice he had letters mailed to him with blank pieces of paper inside. Naturally, there wasn't a return address on the envelope either time. When Johnny told Fergie about these weird occurrences, Fergie seemed thoroughly unconcerned.

"It's just some nut havin' himself a good time," he said nonchalantly. "There's crazies everywhere, an' most of 'em don't hurt anybody—that's what my dad says, anyway."

"Yeah?" Johnny grumbled. "Well, it's not your dad who's getting followed around. What if it's some guy that wants to kidnap me?"

Fergie laughed loudly. "Kidnap you? Good God, Dixon, are you batty? Your gramma and grampa have got about twelve dollars and three cents and a Canadian nickel in the bank."

"Yeah, but my dad has some money," said Johnny stubbornly. Johnny's father was a career officer in the Air Force. Johnny did not get to see him often, but they wrote letters to each other.

Johnny and Fergie argued some more, but Fergie was hard to convince, and he absolutely refused to believe that Johnny was in any kind of danger. Several days passed, and Johnny did not see any blue Fords or get any mysterious midnight phone calls. He decided—reluctantly

—that Fergie was right, and he tried to put his nagging fears behind him. Nothing bad could possibly happen.

August came, and with it, muggy weather and thunderstorms. One rainy night, Johnny sat up late reading and listening to "The Voice of Firestone Hour," a musical program that he liked. On the table near his chair was a plate of crackers spread with pimiento-flavored cream cheese, and now and then Johnny would pause in his reading to grab a cracker and stuff it into his mouth. Rain rattled against the bay window, and thunder muttered and grumbled in the distance. As he turned the pages, Johnny began to realize that he was not paying attention to the story he was reading. Was he bored or just sleepy? He really couldn't tell which. The Sessions clock in the dining room whanged eleven times, and Johnny closed the book. He found that he was thinking about the mysterious snuffbox, which was up in his room. Johnny had been examining it earlier in the day to see if maybe there was some sliding panel on its bottom that would reveal a secret hiding place. But there were no secrets to be found—it was just an empty box. Why did the stupid box fascinate him so much? He had no idea why. Johnny realized that he was getting sleepy. With a sigh, he reached over and turned off the radio and hauled himself to his feet.

When he got to his room, Johnny reached in past the door frame and flipped the light switch, but at that instant there was a horrendous crash of thunder. The lights in the room and the hallway flickered and went out.

"Phooey!" said Johnny. He hated it when the power went out. He could not see very well in the dark, but he groped his way into the room, and his fingers found the old nickel-plated flashlight on top of his bureau. Switching it on, he propped it up with a book so the beam pointed toward him, and then he sat down on the bed and started taking off his shoes. As he undressed, Johnny wondered what had happened to the power. Had a tree limb fallen on a line, or had a car skidded on the wet pavement and rammed a utility pole? Then he wondered if the food in the refrigerator would spoil if the power was off all night. Entertaining himself with thoughts like these, Johnny got his clothes off and put on his pajamas. But just as he was turning to pull down the bedspread, he froze. Out of the corner of his eye he had seen something.

There was a figure crouching on the porch roof outside his bedroom window.

An icy breath of fear blew over Johnny's body. In a flash he knew that the creature was someone who shouldn't be there, someone who *couldn't* be there—it was a visitor from another world. Slowly, Johnny turned to face the thing. The flashlight's beam cast a ghostly sheen on the window, and beyond the glass Johnny saw a fearfully thin shape shuffling forward on his knees. As Johnny watched, rigid with terror, the shadowy form groped at the window . . . and then Johnny blacked out, and he fell in a heap on the floor.

When Johnny woke up, rain was blowing in through the half-open window. Cold drops tickled his face and made him sit up and shake his head violently. Quickly he glanced to his right—the figure was gone. Dragging himself to his feet, Johnny tottered over to the bureau. He began groping with his hands, and at that instant the lights came back on. Johnny blinked and stared. The thing he had been looking for—the snuffbox—was gone. *He came back for it*, Johnny thought. *It was his, and he took it.* Johnny didn't know who *he* was, but he was sure that the shadowy man had come for the snuffbox. He had read somewhere that ghosts could use talismans or magic objects when they wanted to appear to people and warn them about dangers, or do good deeds for them. But once the ghost's mission was accomplished, the talisman had to be returned to the dark void, to the place it had come from. These ghostly rules seemed strange to Johnny, but they made a crazy kind of sense.

Wearily Johnny sat down on the bed, and he tried hard to think. He had an overpowering urge to call up the professor, but he knew how the professor hated being awakened out of a sound sleep, so he resisted the urge. Pounding his forehead with his hand, Johnny forced himself to think: the snuffbox had been sent, and it had been taken away. But why? Apparently the box wasn't important, but the pawn ticket was. So the ghost—or whatever it was—had meant for them to have the sword cane. But what were they supposed to do with it? Stab somebody? Threaten somebody? But who? At this point Johnny's reasoning ran into a stone wall. Then he thought about the blue Ford and the mysterious phone calls. What did they have to do with anything? Johnny pressed his hands to his face, and his head began to throb—all this thinking had gotten him a roaring headache. Wearily, Johnny dragged himself to his feet, and then he went out of the room and down the hall to the bathroom. He took two aspirin tablets and washed them down with a glass of water. He stumbled back to his bed and fell into a dead, dreamless sleep.

The next morning, after breakfast, Johnny decided that he had better go across the street and have a talk with the professor. By now, Johnny was used to bursting in on the professor at any hour of the day or night, so he just trotted up the steps and walked in the front door. He found the professor in the kitchen, having an after-breakfast cigarette and reading the newspaper. As soon as he saw Johnny, the old man put down his newspaper and sat back in his chair, waiting. He knew from the expression on Johnny's face that he had something important to tell him.

"So, John Michael," said the professor cheerfully, "what's on your mind besides hair? Eh?"

Johnny smiled in a sickly way and sank into a chair across the table from the professor. Slowly and hesitantly, with lots of hemming and hawing, he told about the ghost he had seen last night. For good measure, he threw in the tale of the blue Ford and the midnight phone calls. He had not told the professor about these last two things until now, because he had been afraid of being laughed at. It was bad enough to have Fergie razzing him.

When Johnny had finished talking, the professor took his cigarette out of his mouth and thoughtfully ground it out in the remains of the fried egg on his plate. Then he picked up his fork and began stirring the cigarette and the egg together, and as he stirred he talked. "Hmm," said the professor. "John, I hate to say this, but I think you're spooked by a car that you see occasionally, and by some nut who likes to call people up in the middle of the night. It's normal for people to be afraid that they are being followed or persecuted by sinister types—I've had this feeling myself a few times, and each time it's turned out to be my imagination working overtime." The professor paused and pointed his eggy fork at Johnny. "*However*," he said, "that thing you saw outside your window was *not* a product of your imagination. We are dealing with a missioned spirit, a ghost that has come back because there is something it wants us to do. The problem is, we still don't know what the stupid nincompoop of a ghost wants! I think you're right about the snuffbox: it was given to us so we could use the pawn ticket to get the cane. All right—we have the cane. It's out in the umbrella rack in my front hall. Fine. Dandy. But what are we supposed to do with it? Run around sticking people with the sword, until the ghost stops showing up? I'm afraid the ghost just hasn't made its intentions very clear. I've done everything I could, including taking the cane down to the hospital to have the ivory handle X-rayed, just to see if there's anything hidden inside. Well, there isn't—it's solid ivory. So for the time being, I think we'd better try to forget the whole peculiar business and hope that the spirit will go bother somebody else for a change. Do you understand what I'm saying?"

"Uh-huh," said Johnny in a weak, throaty voice. He had expected the professor to have something more helpful to say, and he was feeling disappointed. The professor gave Johnny a searching glance, and he read his thoughts.

"Oh come on, John!" he said, shoving back his chair and standing up suddenly. "Cheer up! It's a nice, filthy hot day in August, and the temperature probably won't get any higher than one hundred and two degrees. So forget your troubles and join me in a nice after-breakfast snack of lemonade and fudge brownies. What d'ye say? Eh?"

CHAPTER FOUR

The rest of August passed, and Labor Day arrived. The professor had a big cookout in his backyard to mark the holiday, and two days later Johnny went back to school. Soon he was all wrapped up in important matters, like the square of the hypotenuse and the fourth principal part of the Latin verb *pello*. The blue Ford and the ghostly midnight visitor faded into the back of Johnny's mind, and his life began to glide along on a fairly even keel. But sometimes, when he was alone in the front hallway of the professor's house, he would take the sword cane out of the umbrella rack and draw the thin, tarnished blade. Then he would mutter *"En garde!"* or "Have at thee, recreant!" and pretend that he was the Count of Monte Cristo or D'Artagnan and lunge and thrust at imaginary enemies.

With a sigh, he would put the sword cane back and wonder—for the five hundredth time—if he would ever know why the ghost had given him this sword. Or had the sword been meant for Fergie? Or the professor? The whole business was so crazy, so nonsensical. Why come back from the dead to give a gift, if nobody knew what the gift was for? As the days of September passed, these questions faded further and further into the back of Johnny's mind, and he began to think that the answers really didn't matter much at all.

One day late in September, Johnny and Fergie were walking home from school together. They were gossiping about their teachers and crabbing about their homework assignments, the way kids often do. As they turned onto Fillmore Street, where Johnny lived, they noticed that about half the leaves were off the trees. In the air hung the smell of burning leaves, but there was another smell too. Johnny's nostrils twitched as he sniffed the odd aroma and tried to figure out what it was.

"That's a funny smell," he said as he glanced around curiously.

Suddenly Fergie lifted his hand and pointed. "Look! *That's* what it is!"

A short way down the street stood the professor's gray stucco house. The professor stood in the driveway burning notebooks and papers. A heap of them was smoldering near his feet and sending up clouds of thick, whitish smoke. The professor reached into the cardboard box he was holding and pitched another fistful of white and blue sheets into the flames. As they drew closer, the boys could see that the expression on the professor's face was unbelievably crabby, and they wondered what had come over him. An odd thought flashed into Johnny's mind: He had often heard the professor say that he would rather burn his students' papers than read them. Maybe at last he had given in to an overwhelming urge. Or perhaps his mind had cracked under the strain of too much teaching—either way, it didn't look good.

With Fergie leading the way, the two boys crossed the street and headed for the gray stucco house. When the professor saw them, he turned and glowered.

"*Well?*" he said fiercely through clenched teeth.

"Hi, prof!" said Fergie, waving cheerfully. He paused and glanced at the box that the professor held in his arms. Then he coughed and forced himself to smile. "Uh . . . whatcha doin'? Huh?"

The professor grimaced and shook a bunch of papers in Fergie's face. "What does it *look* like I'm doing? I'm cleaning out the back room of my study, something that has needed doing for ages. And if you must know, I'm doing this so I won't do something more unpleasant, like throw rocks through my neighbors' windows. The fact is, you see, that I've gotten some bad news."

Johnny's hand flew to his mouth. "Oh, no! What?"

The professor put the box down on the ground, reached into his hip pocket, and pulled out a folded piece of letter paper. "Here," he said, handing the paper to Johnny. "You can read the rotten news for yourself."

With a puzzled expression on his face, Johnny unfolded the note. At the top was an official-looking letterhead that said *M-T Oil Co. San Antonio, Texas*. Beneath this was a brief note:

> To All Stockholders:
>
> M-T Oil Co. regrets that it will be unable to pay any dividends on its stocks until further notice.
>
> > Sincerely,
> > T. Branwell Biggs
> > Chairman of the Board

Johnny gave the professor a puzzled look. "In case you're wondering," growled the professor as he threw more papers onto the fire, "that little message means *We are failing. We are about to go bankrupt.* And ten thousand dollars of my money is going to go bye-bye along with the M-T Oil Company."

Johnny was alarmed. "Is . . . is that all the money you had saved up, professor?"

The professor smiled sourly. "No," he snapped, "but it's a fairly large chunk of it. Up until just recently, I had all my savings in nice, safe securities and bonds. But then I had lunch with this lawyer I know, and he told me that M-T Oil was going to make a major oil strike in the near future, and that I could really clean up if I invested in their stock. Normally, I don't play the stock market, but . . . well, I had this crazy idea that I would make a big wad and then give some to your grandparents, so they wouldn't be so poor. Great plan, wasn't it?"

Johnny was shocked, and his eyes filled with tears. It was true that his gramma and grampa didn't have much money, but his dad would have helped them out if they had gotten into any real financial trouble. He wished that he had told the professor this. Then maybe he wouldn't have . . .

"Don't worry, prof!" said Fergie cheerfully. "They'll probably come up with a gusher, an' then you'll really be in the chips!"

"Fat chance," muttered the professor. Suddenly the professor remembered something. He dug his watch out of his pocket and squinted at it. "However," he said, grinning, "things are not all that bad. In two minutes I have an ooey-gooey chocolate cake coming out of the oven, and I'm going to cover it with great globs of my buttery dark mocha frosting. And if you two are *very* good, you can help me eat some of it. Okay?"

A few minutes later, Fergie and Johnny were sitting at the round oak table in the professor's kitchen. Their mouths were smeared with frosting, and they were attacking huge pieces of cake with their forks. The professor was over by the sink, pouring iced tea into three tall glasses filled with ice cubes. On the drainboard near the glasses was a folded newspaper, and every now and then the professor would peer owlishly at it. Suddenly he let out a loud exclamation.

"Good grief!" he said in an annoyed voice. "The paper says that Cliff Bullard of the Yankees is going to be at the athletic field in Duston Heights on October 15th. Remember the ten thousand smackeroos he's offering to any local boy who can strike him out? Oh, boy! Wouldn't I just *love* to see some big strong kid collect that loot and make Bullard look like the idiot that he is! I tell you, I would drive *miles* to see . . ."

The professor's voice trailed off, and he smiled strangely. A weird and wonderful idea had come floating into his head. Humming quietly, he put the three iced tea glasses on a tray and carried them over to the table. Then he sat down and cut himself a big piece of cake. Johnny and Fergie watched him like hawks—they knew that something was up.

"Okay, prof, what's on your mind?" asked Fergie. "Whenever you get some hotshot idea, you start actin' strange. So come on! Tell us!"

The professor paused with his fork halfway to his mouth. He looked at the two boys uncertainly, as if he really wasn't sure of what he wanted to say. "I know you two will razz me and tell me this is a totally batty idea," he began, "but I was wondering if . . . well, if I could humiliate Cliff Bullard and get back the ten thousand smackers I lost in the stock market at the same time."

Johnny stared. "How the heck could you do that, professor?"

The professor smiled mysteriously. He ate a bite of cake and chewed it slowly. "Easy," he said at last. "All we have to do is find Evaristus Sloane's robot."

Johnny's mouth dropped open, and so did Fergie's. The professor had caught them completely off-guard.

There was an awkward silence. The professor gobbled some more cake and wiped his mouth with his napkin. "You boys think I've flipped my wig, don't you?" he snapped. "Well, I'm as sane as anyone in this room, and I think that the robot still exists. It's probably rusting to pieces in some barn up in New Hampshire, but I'll bet it could be put back together. We could fix the motor and have something that could zip baseballs in at one hundred and ten miles an hour! Bullard would screw himself into the ground trying to hit those pitches!"

Johnny glanced uncomfortably at Fergie. He was really worried about the professor. In the past the old man had come up with some wild notions, but they had always seemed to make some sort of sense. However, this idea made no sense at all. The professor suddenly leaped up and began pacing back and forth.

"I know you're going to ask," he said, "how are we going to win the contest with a robot? Only human beings are allowed to compete in the contest. You were wondering about that, weren't you?"

"I was, kinda," muttered Johnny.

The professor stopped, spun around, and pointed his finger at the boys. "Well, *forget* about your worries!" he said loudly. "I think I have it figured out: the robot really *was* the one that struck out Clutch Klemm back in the old days. I don't know how Sloane made people think the robot was a living, breathing human being, but I'll bet it had something to do with the new source of energy that Sloane discovered."

Johnny was getting more and more bewildered. "Energy source? Professor, you never said anything about that before!"

The professor blinked. "I didn't? I must have left that part out when I told the story. You see, when Sloane rolled his robot out and demonstrated it to the baseball players, no one could figure out how it worked. There wasn't any steam or exhaust smoke pouring out of it, so everyone figured there had to be one of those electric motors inside it. But when Sloane let them see the inside of the robot, the players saw only gears and machinery, no motor! In those days, an electric motor would've been big and heavy, and it would have been hooked up to big heavy batteries or a generator. But there wasn't any such thing in the robot. Well, *something* ran the blasted thing! I can't figure out what this energy source was, but it allowed Sloane to create an illusion when he brought the robot back later. I don't know how he made people think the robot was a man. I don't know how he made the blamed thing run. *That's* what fascinates me! The answer may be hidden away somewhere, gathering dust in a storeroom or an old shed. Doesn't that rouse your spirit of adventure?"

Fergie looked skeptical. "Look, prof," he said slowly, "if this Sloane character really did discover a new source of energy, wouldn't he have sold it to the government for a million bucks?"

The professor shook his head. "No. A sane person would have done that, but Evaristus Sloane was crazy. And he was very, very secretive. He probably decided that nobody *deserved* to know about his wonderful secret. Of course, it's possible that he smashed the robot and burned all his plans. But it's also possible that he didn't."

"Do you know where the robot could be, professor?" asked Johnny timidly.

The professor bit his lip and looked uncertain. "It could be up in Sloane's old house, in New Hampshire—a little bitty burg called Stark Corners. I'm planning to drive up this weekend. You two are welcome to come along, but by golly, if I have to, I'll go alone! Well, what do you yardbirds say?"

Fergie and Johnny looked at each other. They both thought that all this stuff about robots and secret energy sources was looney. But they didn't have anything wonderful planned for the weekend, and they both enjoyed going on car trips with the professor. And the idea appealed to their love of adventure. Even if they only found an old rusting heap of metal that had once been a robot, they would be doing something interesting. After a long pause, Fergie spoke up.

"Prof?"

"Yes, Byron? What is it?"

"Well, uh . . . we wanta have a conference. Johnny and me, that is."

The professor smirked. "A high-level conference! Gracious me, I ought to feel honored to have it held under my roof. Certainly, by all means! Go right ahead!"

The two boys got up and went out to the dining room.

They closed the heavy oak door and talked in low tones for about five minutes, and then they came back. Fergie plunked himself down in a chair, folded his arms, and looked at the professor.

"Okay, prof," he said crisply. "Here's what we decided: We'd like to go along with you, but if we don't find anything right away, we wanta have some fun. You know what I mean?"

The professor smiled sourly. "Gentlemen," he said, "I have no desire to spend the entire weekend prying up floorboards in old barns in New Hampshire. You have my solemn promise: If we don't find anything by Saturday night, we will give up. And then we'll have all day Sunday to cruise around the White Mountains and look at the pretty leaves. But before we go, I'd like to say one thing: I'm not promising you a wonderful adventure. We might end up being bored out of our ever-loving minds. On the other hand, you never can tell—we might uncover some wonderful mystery that has been hidden from the world for a long time."

CHAPTER FIVE

~

The next few days were spent in a flurry of activity as the three travelers got ready for their trip. The professor made reservations at the General Stark Inn, in Stark Corners, and he got his car oiled and gassed up to go. Fergie got permission from his parents to go on the trip— they were happy that he would get a chance to drive up into the White Mountains and see the lovely fall foliage. Johnny's gramma and grampa were also glad that he could go away for a while with his two best friends, the professor and Fergie. So both boys packed and phoned each other up to talk and plan. But they did not say a single word to anyone else about the real purpose of this so-called vacation journey.

Friday afternoon came, and the boys left with the professor in a cloud of exhaust smoke. The skies were black, and it was pouring rain—not great weather for traveling, but as the professor said, it would probably let up sometime. The old maroon Pontiac crawled while the windshield wipers slashed away at the rain, and the boys sang Scouting songs to keep their spirits up. As they drove, the professor tried to point out some scenic spots, like Mount Nancy and Mount Bemis, but they were just vague shapes behind gray veils of rain. Finally, around six in the evening, they pulled into Stark Corners.

There wasn't much to the town: a bandstand on a little patch of grass, some restaurants, two gas stations, a church, a doctor's office, and a few stores. At the far end of the main street stood a two-story white inn with a long front porch. The weathered signboard outside showed a picture of General John Stark, the cantankerous New Hampshireman who had fought in the Revolutionary War.

"Is *this* where we're stayin'?" asked Fergie in a disappointed tone. "It looks like a haunted house."

"It is not in the least like a haunted house," said the professor primly. "It is a very fine old inn that has been in the same family for generations—at least, that is what my guidebook says. Now, come on. Let's drag our suitcases inside and see where they're going to put us."

As the rain pelted down, the professor unlocked the trunk and handed each boy his suitcase. Then he took out his own cracked leather valise and stomped up the creaky steps to the front door. Before he could push the door bell, the door swung open, and there stood a frowning middle-aged woman with a bun of gray hair. She wore a calico apron over her dress, and the apron had flour stains on it.

"Lousy weather ain't it?" she said, and quite suddenly she smiled. The smile made Johnny feel enormously relieved—he was always frightened by crabby people.

"Lousy is the word," said the professor as he stepped inside and shook water off the sleeve of his raincoat. Then he held out his hand. "I'm the Roderick Childermass who called earlier this week. I asked for two rooms for the weekend—a double room for the boys, and a single one for myself. I do hope you've held them for us."

"Pleased to meet you, Mr. Childermass," said the woman, shaking his hand. "I'm Anstis Barnstable. I'm the owner, as you may have guessed. Your rooms are upstairs, and we'll be serving dinner in about twenty minutes. Would you folks like to wash up and get yourselves organized?"

"We would indeed!" said the professor with a satisfied sigh. "Lead on."

A short while later, the professor, Johnny, and Fergie, who were the only guests in the inn, joined Mrs. Barnstable at a table in the long, narrow dining room. Rain pattered at the windows, but inside everything was warm and cozy. A wood stove at one end of the room took away the evening chill, and on the tablecloth were old-fashioned white china plates, tureens, and platters. The meal was a New England boiled dinner: big chunks of beef, potatoes, carrots, and onions swimming in hot broth. The boys dug in greedily, and so did the professor—they hadn't had much to eat for lunch, and they were starved. By the time the dessert was served, the professor was feeling a bit more relaxed and at home, and he decided to shift the conversation to see if he could find out anything about good old Evaristus Sloane.

"Uh . . . wasn't there an inventor who used to live in this town?" he asked casually as he lit his after-dinner cigarette. "Some character named Settle or Sumner or something like that?"

Immediately Mrs. Barnstable stiffened. "Where on earth did you ever hear of *that* awful man?" she asked. "People hereabouts have been trying hard to forget about him."

The professor coughed and glanced away quickly. "Hem! Well, I'm certainly not trying to be nosy, but John's grandfather told him a silly story about a robot that this man had made, and—"

"I hope that's all he told him," said Mrs. Barnstable severely. "There are stories about Evaristus Sloane that are hardly fit for children to hear. He was an evil, twisted person. Do you suppose we can talk about something more pleasant? Boys, would you like another piece of pie? There's plenty in the kitchen."

The professor was surprised. He really hadn't expected to get such a bad reaction when he mentioned the old inventor's name. However, he knew that it wouldn't do to get pushy, so he shrugged and apologized for bringing up such an unpleasant subject. Then, after Mrs. Barnstable had gone to the kitchen, he leaned over and whispered hoarsely to the boys.

"Sounds like old Sloane was a real winner, eh? I knew he was weird, but this lady seems to think he was the devil in human form."

"I guess we better not ask her anything more about him, huh, professor?" said Johnny nervously.

"I suppose not," said the professor. "And we'd better not ask where his house was, unless we want to get tossed out on our ears. Oh, well—we can find out more from somebody else, I suppose."

"You hope," grumbled Fergie. He had been pessimistic about this trip before, and he was even more so now.

After dinner the three travelers went to the parlor to relax. The professor read the paper, and Johnny and Fergie played chess. When ten o'clock came, they were all ready for bed, and they went upstairs and slept soundly. In the morning, when he got up, Johnny saw that the rain had stopped. Sunlight was streaming in through the windows, and little pinkish-gray clouds were drifting over the mountains in the distance. The door to the hall was open, and Johnny could hear the professor singing Latin hymns as he took his morning shower in the bathroom down the hall. Fergie's sheets were rumpled and twisted up at the end of his bed, but he was nowhere to be seen. Probably he was down at breakfast gorging himself—he had always been an early riser. Johnny felt cheerful and optimistic, though he really didn't know why. He whistled and walked around the room several times, and then he slumped into an armchair by the window and started leafing through a copy of *New Hampshire Profiles*, a tourist magazine that he had found lying on the windowsill. Suddenly he stopped turning pages and stared at an article entitled THE HOUSE OF EVARISTUS SLOANE—IS IT HAUNTED? At the top of the page was a pen-and-ink drawing of a stone house built against a cliffside, halfway up a tree-covered mountain.

Johnny swallowed hard. His heart began to beat faster, and the palms of his hands felt sweaty. He tried to read the first sentence of the article, but it was just a blur before his eyes. Then he heard somebody behind him clear his throat.

With a little nervous yelp, Johnny dropped the magazine and leaped out of the chair. He turned and stared wildly at the door, and then he heaved a deep sigh of relief. It was the professor. He was in his bathrobe, and a towel was draped around his neck.

"Good heavens, John!" exclaimed the old man. "Do you always react that way when someone drops by? Calm down! I just wanted to tell you that the bathroom is free whenever you want to use it. Okay?"

Johnny was trembling all over. He opened his mouth to speak, but he could hardly get the words out. "I . . . there's this magazine, and it says . . . it says that . . ."

"Yes?" snapped the professor irritably. "There's a magazine, and it says *what*?"

Instead of answering, Johnny turned and looked down at the place where he had dropped the magazine. But the magazine was gone.

"Oh . . . oh, my gosh . . ." Johnny stammered. He felt cold all over, and he shuddered. "It . . . it was right there, it really was. But now it's gone!"

The professor folded his arms and cocked his head to one side. He pursed his lips skeptically. "John," he said, "are you sure you didn't just fall asleep in your chair? What's all this nonsense about a magazine that isn't there?"

Johnny got more flustered than ever. He stooped and tilted the armchair sideways. But there was nothing under it. With a sad look the professor walked across the room and put his hand gently on Johnny's arm.

"John," he said quietly, "you must have had a little dream when you dozed off in the armchair a few minutes ago. Now scoot on down the hall and brush your teeth while I get into some clothes. This looks like a beautiful day, and we're all going to go exploring."

Johnny's mind was in a whirl. Could the professor possibly be right? Were the magazine and the article just a dream? But he had been wide awake when he found the magazine—he was very sure of that. On the other hand, it would not do to argue with the professor. So Johnny just shrugged his shoulders helplessly and started on down the hall toward the bathroom.

After breakfast, Fergie, Johnny, and the professor left the inn and took a short walk down the main street of the town. They stopped at a variety store and bought a newspaper and some candy bars. While the boys stood around looking at comic books, the professor tried to get some information out of the owner of the store.

"Have you ever heard of this Evaristus Sloane character?" he asked as he lit a black and gold cigarette. "You know, the nutty inventor?"

The owner frowned. "Yes, I have," he said sourly. "What about him?"

The professor hemmed and hawed. "Oh, well . . . you see, the fact is, I'm writing a book on old New Hampshire legends, and I want to do a little piece on Sloane. Is it true he used to live in Stark Corners?"

The owner grunted. "Not exactly *in* the town. He lived in a house halfway up Mount Creed, which is the big mountain that kinda hangs over the town. You go outa town 'bout half a mile on Burnt Mill Road, an' there's this dirt road that leads on up the mountain. If you take my advice, you'll leave your car down at the bottom—road's not in too great a shape. Anyways, the house is 'bout a half hour walk up the road. It's all closed up an' fallin' to pieces, an' if you want some more advice, I wouldn't hang around after sunset."

The professor stared. "Why not?"

The owner gave the professor a quick, nervous glance. "Well, there's a lot o' broken boards an' nails in the yard, an' there's an old cistern with a wooden cover that's all rotted out. You might fall in an' hurt yerself. Y'know what I mean?"

The professor stared harder. There was something

about the way the owner was acting that was very creepy and unnerving. "Humph!" snorted the professor as he stubbed his cigarette out in an ashtray that stood on the counter. "Well, thank you for the advice and the directions." He turned and motioned toward Johnny and Fergie. "Come on, boys. We've got a little car ride and a hike ahead of us."

The boys grinned and put the comic books back in the rack. Then they followed the professor out the door and down the sidewalk toward the inn.

"I hate people who won't give you a straight answer," grumbled the professor as they walked along. "If the old fool thinks there are any ghosts up at Sloane's house, why the blue blazes doesn't he *say* so? Nails, my foot! Rotten cistern cover! He just didn't have the decency to say what he meant!"

Maybe he thought you'd laugh at him, thought Johnny. He was still unhappy about the way the professor had brushed off his story about the disappearing magazine.

When they arrived at the inn, Fergie and Johnny waited downstairs while the professor went up to his room and got his camera, pocket compass, and sunglasses.

"All right, boys!" he said as he shoved the camera into Fergie's hands. "Are you ready to inspect that nest of spooks and spectres?"

Fergie and Johnny nodded, and they all got into the car. The engine roared, and off they went. When they were about a half mile out of town, the professor slowed down and started looking for the place where they were supposed to turn off. As they rounded a curve, they saw it: a rutty little dirt road running up into the trees that covered the mountain. The professor swerved the car left, and they started bouncing and jolting up the mountain road. Fergie was in the backseat. He leaned forward and started talking into the professor's ear.

"Hey, prof," he said, "I don't like to crab, but didn't that guy in the store say we shouldn't try to drive up this road?"

"Yeah," said Johnny, who was sitting up in front next to the professor. "I think he did say that."

"I *know* what the man said!" the professor muttered testily. "But for the time being, the road seems passable, and—"

The professor's little speech was interrupted by a loud musical *bonggg*! A rock had hit the underside of the car. But the professor did not stop. He drove on, and the car jolted and jounced, and the springs squealed and complained. Finally, after a few twists and turns, the road became totally impossible: it turned into a pair of ruts with boulders jutting up here and there, and even the professor could see that driving on was useless. With a muttered curse, he pulled off onto a sandy shoulder, and they all got out.

It was a good morning for a hike. The sun was shining, and the maple trees were aflame with red and yellow and orange leaves. For half an hour they slogged up the steep, rocky road. Finally they came to a little meadow full of tall bearded grass and purple pieweed. And there was the house. It was made of yellowish sandstone, and it had a steep-pitched roof and narrow, pointed gables. The place looked utterly abandoned: the downstairs windows were boarded up, and the porch sagged. As they trudged across the meadow toward the house, Johnny tripped over a square board that lay hidden in the grass. It was a weathered FOR SALE sign.

"I'm not surprised they had trouble selling this dump," said the professor as he glanced at the sign. "You'd have to be a little dotty to want to live up here the year round. Can you imagine how lonely it would be in the winter? And it's much too grim and gloomy to be a vacation home." He gave the sign a little kick and walked on toward the house.

For some reason, nobody wanted to go in right away. The professor snapped pictures and chattered about old houses, and Johnny picked pieweed stalks and then threw them away. Whenever they stopped talking, the oppressive silence of the place began to make them feel nervous, and they would start talking again. As the sun rose higher, the three of them circled around into the yard that lay on the north side of the house. Suddenly, Fergie raised his hand and pointed at something. In the middle of the sloping roof was a tiny square window.

"Hey, look at that!" he said. "That's a heck of a funny place for a window, isn't it?"

"I've seen them before," said the professor as he

squinted up into the sun. "They put them there to let more light into the attic. Speaking of which, I suppose that's the first place we ought to look. How about it, kids? Are you ready for a little breaking and entering?"

Johnny started getting fidgety. He was always terrified of doing something illegal, but he didn't want Fergie to think he was chicken. However, when he glanced at Fergie, he saw that he was looking nervous too. *There's something about the house that he doesn't like*, thought Johnny. But he said nothing.

The professor glowered at the boys. "Look, you two!" he growled, "are you coming or not? Byron, you're the one who always loves exploring, aren't you? Well, here's your chance! Am I going to have to go charging in there by myself?"

Fergie looked at Johnny, and he smiled weakly. "C'mon, big John," he said, with a half-hearted wave of his hand. "Let's go search for robots an' stuff. Okay?"

"Okay," muttered Johnny, and he started walking slowly toward the house.

There wasn't any problem about getting in—the lock on the front door was broken, and the door hung slightly ajar. With the professor in the lead, the three of them stepped inside the old house and began walking through the empty and desolate rooms. Pieces of plaster had fallen from the ceiling here and there, and flies buzzed and bumped against the dirty windows. They started up the stairs. On the second floor they found a door that led to a narrow staircase, and they climbed it too. The attic was as empty as the rest of the house. An old-fashioned light socket hung from one of the rafters, and there was a small, floor-level window at the far end of the room. But there was nothing up there, no robot, not even a stick of broken furniture.

"Phooey!" said the professor. "Double phooey, with cheese and tartar sauce!" Stooping, he ran his fingertip over the floorboards, and then he examined the tip of his finger. "You know what's funny?" he went on in a thoughtful voice. "This place is a lot cleaner than you would expect it to be. There isn't any junk lying around—no beer bottles or moldy half-eaten sandwiches, or things of that sort. Usually hoboes camp out overnight in abandoned houses like this one. But I don't see any sign that they have."

"Maybe they didn't feel welcome here," said Johnny in a strange voice.

The professor looked at him for a second and opened his mouth to say something. But at this point Fergie interrupted.

"Hey, prof!" he said, jabbing his finger into the professor's arm. "I'll tell you somethin' else that's screwy: I can't see that little roof window anywhere. Wouldn't it be right up over our heads?"

The professor was startled. He thought a bit, and then he began to smile. There was a gleam in his eyes. "Ye-es . . ." he said slowly. "The window *would* be over our heads, unless . . . unless . . ."

"Unless there's another attic room!" said Johnny excitedly.

"Precisely," said the professor. "Pree-*cisely*! And now I think we had better go see if we can find a way to get into it. Are you coming, gentlemen?"

CHAPTER SIX

⧉

The professor and the two boys went down to the second floor of the house, and they started going through the rooms. It didn't take them long to find what they were looking for. In a bedroom in the northeast corner of the house, they saw the outline of a door under the faded pink wallpaper. Eagerly they went to work ripping away the paper, and when they were through, there was an old paneled door. The knob was gone and the keyhole was filled with putty, but when the professor gave the door a kick, it groaned and moved inward. Eddies of dust sifted down from the top of the door frame. He kicked harder, and the door flew back with a loud, alarming clatter. Behind the door lay a shallow closet, and a ladder was bolted to the back wall. At the top of the ladder, set in the ceiling, was a small trapdoor.

"Well, well!" said the professor, putting his hands on his hips. "It looks as if we have struck pay dirt! Who wants to go up first?"

Fergie said that he had the right to go first, since he had been the one who noticed the window in the roof. The professor grinned and stepped back, and Fergie started to climb. When he got to the top of the ladder, he reached up and shoved at the trapdoor. It was loose, so Fergie gave it a hard push, and it went flying back. More dust and a stale, shut-up smell came drifting down through the small square opening. Fergie climbed up another rung and poked his head into the room above.

"Oh, my gosh!" he exclaimed in an awestruck voice. "Hey, you guys, it's up here! It really is! The robot—the whole darned thing!"

Johnny was overjoyed. He felt like dancing and yelling, and he could see that the professor was pretty tickled too. They were like archeologists who had discovered King Tut's tomb.

"Wonderful!" crowed the professor, rubbing his hands with glee. "Byron, climb on up into the room. John, you can go up next if you want to."

A few minutes later, all three of them were kneeling on the floor of the tiny attic room. Overhead, a thick pane of lead-colored glass let a faint light seep in. Lying in a heap against the wall were the pieces of the wonderful baseball-throwing robot. Its arms lay stacked on its headless body, and its legs stood against the wall. The wheeled platform was propped against a rafter, and nearby, on a little shelf, stood the robot's head. It stared weirdly out into the room, but the stare was blank—the robot's eyes were gone.

Humming quietly, the professor picked up one of the robot's arms and examined it. It was the cast-iron throwing arm, and it was quite heavy. "Interesting," muttered the professor. "He had the arm coated with zinc, so there really isn't much rust. I brought my toolbox with me in the car, and I'll bet I could get this silly gizmo slapped back together and in working order in no time."

Fergie glanced quickly at Johnny, and Johnny winced. He knew what Fergie was thinking: The professor was always bragging about how good he was with tools, but everybody knew that he could hardly drive a nail straight. If he tried putting the robot together, they might be up here in New Hampshire for a long, long time.

The professor glowered. "Well, what are you two simpering and snickering about? Hmm? I fixed the windshield wipers on my car the other day, and they worked . . . for a while, anyway. If either of you thinks he can put the robot together faster, go right ahead."

Fergie gave Johnny another look, and then he coughed and tried to smile in a reassuring way. "Prof," he began, "we . . . we know you're a real whiz with tools an' all, but . . . well, doncha think we ought to take the pieces of this whatchamajigger back with us in the car? We could get a real . . . er, I mean some car repair man to screw it back together for us. It probably wouldn't cost much, would it?"

The back of the professor's neck began to get red, which was a sign that he was becoming irritated. "Gentlemen," he said in a biting tone, "I was not planning to do the whole job of reassembling the robot up here. I thought I would merely, well, screw the head onto the body and have a look at the machinery inside the chest cavity. Then we could carry the pieces of the robot down to my car and take it to my basement workshop at home. And I wish you two would stop giving each other funny looks. I'm a perfectly reasonable person, and I'm not all *that* bad with tools. Now, why don't you two help me carry the pieces of our friend here downstairs, and then I'll go get my toolbox and we'll see what can be done. Okay?"

Fergie and Johnny shrugged helplessly. The professor climbed halfway down the ladder, and the boys handed pieces of the robot down to him through the trapdoor hole. Except for the cast-iron arm, the pieces were surprisingly light, and the professor remarked that the robot might be made of aluminum.

"*Aluminum?*" said Fergie in a surprised voice. "Did they have aluminum way back then?"

The professor nodded. "They did indeed! There's a statue in Piccadilly Circus in London that's made of aluminum, and it was put there in 1893. Anything else you'd like to know? Hmm?"

A little while later, all the pieces of the robot were lying on the grass in the field next to the house. The professor was kneeling next to the shiny metal body, and he was peering in through a little door in the man's chest.

"Mercy!" he said, shaking his head in despair. "It looks like the night they went crazy at the clock factory! I've never seen so many gears and levers in my born days!" With a sigh, he shut the metal door and stood up. "And there's another thing," he went on, rubbing his chin thoughtfully. "I wonder what happened to the eyes? People claimed they were extremely lifelike—made of glass, probably. Oh, well. The eyes were just ornaments, and I'm wasting time yammering on like this. You boys stay here—I'll scoot on down to the car and get my toolbox, and we'll see what can be done."

The professor walked off across the field humming quietly.

"Well, we found the famous gizmo," said Fergie as soon as the professor was out of sight. "I hope the prof is happy. But I still don't see how he's gonna pass this hunk of junk off as a real human being."

"I don't either," said Johnny glumly. He looked down at the pieces of the robot that lay shining in the sunlight. "But he said there was this energy source that made the robot go, and maybe that's the answer. Maybe the mysterious energy source made the robot look like a real person. Could that be possible?"

Fergie shrugged. "Search me! All I know is, this 'energy source' stuff sounds like a lot of garbage. Does he think that old whosis came up with atomic power back in the horse and buggy days? That's kinda hard to believe!"

Johnny said nothing. The robot was a riddle, but he knew one thing: He would be very glad to get away from this place. The house was grim and forbidding, even in the daytime. Idly, Johnny watched a bird fly by. Then he stretched and yawned and walked around picking pieweed stalks. Fergie sat down on a rotting stump and took a harmonica out of his shirt pocket. He began to play an old sad folk tune. Johnny knew the words:

> Come all you young fellows so young and so fine
> And seek not your fortune in a dark dreary mine
> For 'twill form as a habit and seep in your soul
> Till the stream of your blood is as black as the coal
> For it's dark as a dungeon and damp as the dew
> And the sorrows are many and the pleasures but few . . .

Fergie played on, and Johnny walked away with his bunch of flowery purple plants. He was looking for a jar or a bucket to stick them in, and he had a vague idea that there might be one out behind the house. As he walked, he began to feel very odd. It seemed to him that the air had suddenly gotten chilly. And the sound of the harmonica grew fainter, as if Fergie were playing off in some distant place. Dreamily Johnny turned and stared at an old rusty drainpipe that ran down the back side of the house. Sure enough, there was a coffee can full of water under the drainpipe. He started to walk toward it, but he hadn't taken two steps when something made him turn.

Not far from the back door of the house stood a bench covered with peeling white paint. It was a garden seat, the kind people used to make so they could sit outdoors on hot summer nights. The bench stood in a patch of wild rosebushes not far from the rugged wall of the mountain, which towered overhead. A man was sitting on the bench —a man Johnny had never seen before. He wore baggy, dusty overalls and a faded plaid shirt, and he had a big mop of straw-colored hair. The man sat hunched over with his face in his hands, and he seemed to be crying. Johnny stood dead still. The bunch of pieweed stalks fell from his numb fingers, and he took a couple of shuffling steps forward. And then, as Johnny watched, the man stood up. He took his hands away from his face and he stumbled. Johnny gasped in terror—the man had no eyes. Streaks of blood ran down from empty black sockets.

"They took my eyes," the man moaned. "They took my eyes."

Johnny opened and closed his mouth, and made little whimpering noises. He shut his eyes tight to block out this horrible vision, and when he opened them again a second later, the man was gone.

CHAPTER SEVEN

Johnny was so frightened that he couldn't even scream. He stood staring, eyes wide, at the empty bench and the patch of grass where the man had been standing. He hadn't had time to run away—Johnny's eyes hadn't been closed that long. Who or what had he seen? Was it the ghost whose voice he had heard at the old baseball stadium? And was this the same creature that had appeared to him as a scrawny shadow crouching outside his bedroom window? Johnny raised his hand and found that it was trembling violently. In the distance, Fergie's mournful harmonica music went on endlessly. After swallowing several times and licking his dry lips, Johnny found his voice.

"Fergie? F-Fergie?" he said weakly. Then he pulled

air into his lungs and bellowed: *"Fergie! Fergie! Help! Quick!"*

The harmonica-playing stopped, and soon Fergie was galloping across the grass to the place where Johnny stood. "Yeah? What . . . what is it, John baby?" gasped Fergie breathlessly.

Johnny was still so shaken that he had trouble putting words together. "I . . . oh, my gosh, Fergie, I saw . . . oh, you'll never believe what I saw," Johnny stammered, and he pointed a trembling finger at the bench. "He . . . a guy . . . he was right there . . . a man with no eyes . . . it was awful!"

Fergie was astonished—he really didn't know what to say. "You mean it was a ghost?" he asked, frowning skeptically. "Is that what you think you saw?"

Johnny glared. "It's not what I *think* I saw, it's what I *saw*! I'm not crazy, Fergie, and I'm tellin' you that right there, five minutes ago, there was this—"

"Yes? Yes? What is it? What in heaven's name is going on here?"

Fergie and Johnny turned. There stood the professor, red-faced and out of breath. He had been walking up the road with his tool kit when he heard Johnny yell, and he had come pounding pell-mell across the field to see what was the matter. Patiently Johnny told the story of what he had seen. Now that he was calmer, he could give more details and make more sense. The professor listened with a grave expression on his face. Johnny couldn't tell if he believed him or not.

"That is a very strange tale," said the professor in a hushed voice. "I have no doubt that it's the ghost that gave you the snuffbox, the one that has visited you twice before. But why he should have come to you now, in this place, I can't imagine. However, speaking of mysterious occurrences, let me tell you what happened to me a few minutes ago: I was on my way back to the car, when I happened to turn my head, and I saw a bluejay pecking at something that was caught in a bush. I was curious, so I went over and chased the bird away, and guess what I found? An old-fashioned case that was meant to hold a pair of spectacles. But there were no spectacles inside. Instead, well . . . here, let me show you what I found."

The professor knelt down and opened the toolbox. From it he took the case he had been talking about, and he popped it open. Inside were two glass eyes.

Johnny turned pale. Once again, he seemed to hear the moaning words of the ghostly figure: *They took my eyes . . . they took my eyes.*

"Now, what do you make of all this?" said the professor, giving each of the boys a searching look. "I will bet you fifty dollars that these are the eyes that belong in the robot we found. Somebody must have stolen the case from the house, and when the robber found out what was inside, he threw it away. I suppose that if we had any brains we would throw these disgusting objects and the robot away too. *However*, I have never been known for being sensible, so I am going ahead with my plan. Do I hear any strong objections from anybody?"

Johnny and Fergie looked at each other. They both could see that something uncanny was going on here, but —like the professor—they were not going to be scared away. Silently the three of them went back to the place where the pieces of the robot were lying. The professor got some screws and a screwdriver out of the toolbox and bolted the head onto the body of the robot. With the help of the boys, the professor lugged the armless and legless figure down to the car. They put it in the trunk, and then went back for the other parts. When all the pieces of the robot were in the trunk, the professor revved up the engine and made a screeching, lurching U-turn. As the car bumped away down the road, Fergie threw an anxious glance at Johnny, who was sitting in the backseat. He looked very pale and frightened.

"Prof?" Fergie asked. "How come you didn't put the eyes back in the robot?"

The professor grimaced. "Because I did not want to stir up any evil forces that may be lurking near the old house," he said. "When we're back in Duston Heights, there will be time for putting all the parts of the robot back together, and I hope that we will also be able to figure out what makes it run. But I'll let you in on a little secret, Byron: If it turns out that there is no secret energy source, and this is just a tin man full of gears and rods, I will not be too unhappy. We can donate the machine to a museum and forget about striking out Cliff Bullard. It was a pretty silly idea, anyway. Now that I've seen the robot, I realize that it couldn't possibly have been used in that contest.

There's no way it could have been mistaken for a living, breathing human being."

"You better hope there's no way," muttered Fergie as he thought about the heap of metal parts that clunked and clattered in the trunk of the professor's car.

When they got back to the General Stark Inn, the professor went inside and explained to Mrs. Barnstable that he and the boys were going to have to cut their vacation trip short. He claimed that Johnny had come down with a bad cold and would need to be put to bed at home as soon as possible. Mrs. Barnstable was very sympathetic, and she even refused the extra money the professor offered her. So while Johnny stayed in the car and pretended to be ill, Fergie and the professor went upstairs, packed all the bags, and brought them down. Mrs. Barnstable came out onto the porch of the inn and waved good-bye as they drove off. When they got back to Duston Heights, the boys helped the professor carry the pieces of the robot down to his basement workshop.

Days passed. Johnny and Fergie went back to their normal everyday routine of school, homework, and hanging around Peter's Sweet Shop. In the evenings, they usually dropped by the professor's house to see how he was doing with the robot. It was funny to watch him pretending to be a handyman: he would dress in old jeans and a red flannel shirt, and he would take measurements and talk about screw eyes and wing bolts, but it was pretty obvious that he didn't have the faintest idea of what he was doing. Slowly the robot got put together, and the professor's fingers got covered with Band-Aids. One day, about a week after the trip to New Hampshire, he called up Johnny and Fergie and told them that the robot was all assembled, except for the glass eyes. He wanted them to come down and see the eyes put in, and they would have a modest little celebration, with chocolate cake and champagne. Grampa and Gramma Dixon were invited too, and they said that they would come. Grampa was very interested in seeing the robot, and also a little bit scared—he remembered the way he had reacted when he first saw the robot, fifty years before.

At nine o'clock that evening, everybody was down in the basement workshop, munching homemade fudge cake and sipping cheap New York State champagne. In the middle of the room stood the robot. It was mounted on its metal platform, and it looked very odd indeed: the outside was sculpted to look like a baseball player in uniform, and the pinstripes of the player's shirt and pants were painted red. On the head was a metal baseball cap with a large *S* (for Spiders) stamped on the front, and under the creature's nose was a curling metal mustache. One arm hung limp, but the other—the throwing arm—was cocked back, ready to fire. The empty eyes seemed to stare unpleasantly at the people who milled about, sizing the robot up.

"It's certainly an amazing gizmo," said the professor, waving his fork at the robot. "And what is most amazing is this: I can't for the life of me figure out how old Sloane made it work! All the gears and things inside it are in their proper place, but the motor's missing. There isn't even any place—as far as I can see—where the silly motor was mounted! And yet, *something* made it run. Didn't he demonstrate the thing for your team, Henry?"

"That's right, Rod," said Grampa, nodding. "The darned whatchamajigger threw like Cy Young. It was like shootin' a baseball out of a cannon! But when we asked Sloane what made the thing go, he laughed an' said that the power source was a secret."

The professor made a puckery face. "It's certainly a well-kept secret," he said dryly. "I suppose there must have been an electric motor inside the thing, and then later he managed to wipe out all traces of it. Weird, eh?" With a loud harrumph, the professor put his champagne glass down and went over to his workbench. There lay the spectacle case that held the two glass eyes. Silence fell, and everyone who was standing near the robot stepped back a pace or two.

"Now, then," said the professor with a nervous cough. He moved toward the robot, stood up on tiptoe, and took a tube of rubber cement from his shirt pocket. After putting just a little dab of cement in each socket, he took the eyes out of their holder and pressed them into place. Then he stepped back, and the people who were watching applauded. It was faint, polite applause, because everybody was nervous. They all expected something strange to happen when the eyes were put in. The robot stared blankly ahead, but that was all. He did not even look terribly real, the way wax figurines sometimes do.

"So there!" said the professor as he wiped his gluey fingers on a cloth. "I'm disappointed in a way—I almost thought old Ziggy there would step down off his pedestal and have a drink with us."

Everybody laughed, and immediately the party got a great deal more relaxed. Johnny and Fergie went over into a corner and started playing a pinball machine, and the three older people went upstairs to the living room, so they could sit and talk. After a half-dozen games, the two boys got bored with pinball and decided to go upstairs. Fergie turned and took one more look at the robot. He looked thoughtful and a bit disappointed.

"Y'know, John baby," he said, "that tin pitcher isn't nearly as scary as I thought it'd be. I had kinda made up my mind that there'd be some energy source in those eyes, an' they'd make the thing start wavin' its arms or somethin'."

Johnny was surprised. Fergie was usually the calm, logical type, and when he had weird ideas, he tried to hide them. "Why the heck did you think *that* would happen?" asked Johnny with a little giggle. "I think you've been readin' too many science-fiction comic books."

Fergie made no answer. He just shrugged and started up the stairs, and Johnny followed. They went to the living room, where the professor was just beginning to play "The Star-Spangled Banner" on his upright piano. This was the way he always let his guests know that the party was over. Fergie went home, and Johnny trotted back across the street with Gramma and Grampa. The two old people went upstairs to bed, but Johnny wasn't sleepy yet, so he wandered into the living room and turned on the TV set. Then he went out to the kitchen and made himself a pimiento-cheese sandwich and poured a glass of ginger ale. He had just gotten back to the living room when he was startled by a terrific loud pounding. Putting his glass and plate down on the coffee table, Johnny rushed to the door. There stood the professor in his bathrobe and pajamas. His glasses were stuck onto his face crookedly, and his hair was wild. He looked absolutely frightful.

"John! John!" gasped the old man as he staggered into the front hall. "It's gone! The robot's gone! Oh, my lord, what are we going to do? What on *earth* are we going to do?"

CHAPTER EIGHT

Johnny was thunderstruck. All sorts of wild ideas came rushing into his head. "You . . . you mean somebody stole it?"

The professor shook his head miserably. "No, no! That's *not* what I mean! No one could possibly have . . . but wait! If you'll come across the street with me, you'll see what I mean. Come on!"

With a dazed look on his face, Johnny followed the professor across the street and into his house. The door to the cellar was in the kitchen, and before he opened it the professor paused and tapped the dead-bolt lock with his finger. "This door is the only way into the basement, except the windows," he said. "And there's no sign that any of the basement windows has been forced open. After you folks left, I spent about an hour here in the kitchen, doing dishes. Once or twice I went to the living room to poke the fire in the fireplace, but I would certainly have heard anyone who tried to drag the robot up the cellar stairs. But the blasted thing is gone! Have you ever heard of anything like that in your life?"

Opening the cellar door, the professor stepped aside and waved Johnny ahead. Down the creaky steps he went, and at the bottom he paused. All the lights were on, and he could see the professor's workbench and the bare place on the cement floor where the robot had stood. Johnny began to feel faintly sick inside. This was the kind of eerie unexplainable thing that he had feared.

"Hard to believe, isn't it?" muttered the professor as he began turning the lights out. "Something very uncanny is going on, and I'm afraid this may be just the beginning of our troubles. *Where* do you suppose that miserable hunk of tin has gone to?"

Johnny didn't have any answers. He went upstairs and sat around in the kitchen talking to the professor for a while, and then he went home. When he finally went to bed, he did not get much sleep, and when he came stumbling down to breakfast the next morning, he found Grampa sitting at the kitchen table with a newspaper in his hand. He looked shocked.

"Oh . . . hullo, Johnny," said Grampa in a distracted way. "I was just readin' in the paper—somethin' awful happened here in town last night! I never heard of anythin' like it, not ever!"

Johnny grew tense. Vague, shapeless fears began to form in his mind. "What . . . what is it, Grampa?" he asked.

The old man handed Johnny the newspaper. It was the Duston Heights *Gazette*, and on the front page was a headline: SENSELESS BEATING SHOCKS CITY. Underneath was an article, and Johnny began to read it:

> At a little after midnight last night, Officer Paul Willard was passing the home of Mrs. Anna Tremblay, of 306 South Cedar Street. He noticed that the front door of the Tremblay home was open, swinging in the wind, and the screen door had been ripped from its hinges—it lay halfway down the front walk. Stopping to investigate, Officer Willard entered the house, called out, and when he received no reply, began to search. On the floor of the living room he found Mrs. Tremblay lying unconscious. Her face and body were badly bruised, and under her fingernails were bits of red paint. Mrs. Tremblay is an elderly widow, and according to neighbors, she seldom receives visitors. She has not yet regained consciousness, so the identity of her assailant remains a mystery. Nothing of any value had been taken from the Tremblay house, and this has led observers to say that the intruder must have been an escaped lunatic. . . .

Johnny looked up. All the color had drained from his face. He was thinking of the painted red pinstripes on the robot's body.

"Ain't that the most awful thing you ever heard of?" asked Grampa. "This is s'posed t'be a safe town where nobody ever locks their doors. Well, I'll betcha they start lockin' 'em now!"

Johnny nodded. Suddenly he felt alarmed—he didn't see Gramma anywhere. At this hour of the morning, she was usually puttering around in the kitchen.

"Where's Gramma?" he asked nervously.

Grampa smiled. "Oh, she's down the street talkin' to Mrs. Kovacs 'bout the break-in. Wants t'find out all the gory details. You oughta go over an' talk to the professor 'bout this—he's always playin' Sherlock Holmes an' tryin' t'outguess the police. I'll betcha he's got some theories already!"

I'll bet he does, thought Johnny grimly. He wanted to tell Grampa about the robot's disappearance, but last night the professor had made him promise not to tell anyone what had happened. Johnny felt helpless, and he felt frightened. If the robot could pass through locked doors and walls and beat up old Mrs. Tremblay, he could come back to Fillmore Street and hurt Gramma and Grampa. Johnny wanted very much to go across the street and talk to the professor, but he was a bit scared to: when the professor got bad news, he flew into a rage—he broke crockery and punched holes in plaster walls. Johnny did not want to be around when the professor started raging.

While he was trying to make up his mind what to do, he heard a loud *vrrrrrROOM!* Johnny rushed to the front door, and he was just in time to see the professor's car come peeling out into the street at an incredible speed. Then, with a grinding of gears and a squealing of tires, the car shot off down Fillmore Street. The professor had probably gone to see his old friend, Professor Charles Coote of the University of New Hampshire. Johnny didn't know for sure that this was what he was doing, but he felt fairly certain—Professor Coote was an expert on black magic and ghosts, and it was possible that he would be able to help them do something about the robot. Johnny was a bit hurt that the professor hadn't wanted to take him along, but he knew that there were some things that the old man wanted to do alone. Oh, well—there was always Fergie. Johnny wanted to have a long talk with him about this whole strange business. Of course, he would have to break his promise to the professor, but Johnny was not always perfect when it came to keeping promises.

The professor was away all day. Meanwhile, Johnny and Fergie walked the streets of Duston Heights and talked about the mysterious robot with the glass eyes. Both of them were convinced that the robot had attacked old Mrs. Tremblay, but that was about the only thing they agreed on.

"How about that! The darned thing is *magic*!" muttered Fergie thoughtfully. "Magic is what makes it run, and not some super-duper energy source. But nothin' happened till after the prof stuck the eyes back in the robot's head. So I was right about those glass eyes after all! The prof shoulda been more careful—he should never of stuck those eyes back in the darned thing's head."

"How did he know anything was gonna happen?" asked Johnny, irritably. "I mean, he's not a wizard or anything. He just thought—"

"Well, he should've thought some more!" snapped Fergie. "Now that darned pile o' tin is out there runnin' around, clobberin' people! Where do you think it is now? Any idea?"

Johnny shrugged and kicked a stone down the street. "Fergie, how would *I* know? Maybe it hitched a ride to Kansas City! It's out there on the loose, an' we have to stop it. That's why the professor went up to see Mr. Coote, so he could—"

"Are you sure that's where he went?" asked Fergie in a taunting voice. "Maybe he's tryin' to get out of the country so the cops won't arrest him for what happened to Mrs. Whatsis."

Johnny turned on Fergie angrily. "Look, Fergie, the professor's not a coward! He didn't know he was gonna start that robot goin', but I know he's sure gonna try to stop it. I bet you he'll be home tonight. Come on over after dinner an' we can go see him. Okay?"

Fergie's mouth curled into a sarcastic smile. "All right, I'll be over," he said. "But I'll bet you fifty cents the prof doesn't have any answers when he comes back. That old geezer up in New Hampshire doesn't know everything.

An' he sure won't know how to handle that crummy robot!"

"He won't, huh? Okay, I'll take your bet—you pay me fifty cents if Professor Coote doesn't know what to do about the robot."

That evening, when the professor's old maroon Pontiac pulled up in front of his house, Fergie and Johnny were sitting on the front porch. The car door slammed, and the old man got out. Under his arm he carried a thick book bound in peeling blue leather. He seemed very tired, and he trudged slowly up the walk with his head down. But when he saw the boys, he managed a weary smile.

"Well, gentlemen!" he said sighing. "It seems I have a welcoming committee. Greetings! I've just gotten back from visiting my old pal Charley Coote, and—as you may have guessed—we talked about the robot. We—"

"Did you find out what to do?" asked Johnny eagerly. "To stop the thing, I mean?"

The professor sighed and patted the book under his arm. "Did I find out what to do? Yes, and no. There are some answers in here, but they don't seem terribly helpful. Come on inside and I'll show you what I mean."

A few minutes later, the two boys were sitting at the professor's kitchen table. They were drinking Coke and staring at the huge old book that was spread out before them. It was written in Latin, but the professor was standing behind the boys, and as they listened he began to read the book aloud, in English:

"How you may make a statue that will work for you: Take the eyes from a living human and pack them in myrrh, cassia bark, and aloes, and then say over the eyes the prayer of Cagliostro and offer incense to Asmodai. After forty days the eyes will become like glass and may be used to make a statue come to life. Be warned! *Do not* place the eyes in the head of the statue until you have made the Key of Arbaces. The key will allow you to control the living statue. Without it, the creature will become wild and uncontrollable, and in the end it will murder you, its creator, if it can find you. By using the key properly, you can make the statue do tasks for you, pass through walls of stone and steel, and even kill those whom you hate. I will add that—"

The professor stopped reading. "Well, there you are, boys!" he said, sourly. "Isn't that a lovely set of instructions for would-be wizards to follow? Charley Coote says that this book is a fairly common one—Evaristus Sloane must have had a copy. So now we know how he brought the robot to life. *Brrh!* What an awful thing to do! He must have killed the man whose eyes he stole, and that was the man's ghost that you saw, John. Evil, evil man— Evaristus Sloane, I mean. No wonder the lady at the inn didn't want to talk about him!"

Fergie turned in his seat and looked up at the professor. "Prof?" he asked. "Do you know what this Key of Whosis is? The one that controls the robot?"

The professor scowled. "No. There are no instructions

in the book about how to make such a key. Charley says that the Key of Arbaces must have been one of those things that wizards learned about when they took lessons from other wizards. The instructions were probably never written down."

"Oh, great!" exclaimed Fergie. "Just great! So how are we gonna stop the robot if we can't make one of those keys?"

"How indeed?" sighed the professor. "Charley and I discussed this problem for a long time. We even talked about the sword cane that the ghost sent us, but neither of us can figure out how it can be of any use to us. I mean, a sword is a sword and a key is a key. Sooo . . . we think that we'll just have to find the key that Sloane used. There are two places where it might be hidden: one is in his grave."

"His *grave?*" said Johnny, and he made an awful face.

The professor nodded solemnly. "Yes. As far as I know, Sloane is dead, so—as disgusting as it is to think about— we may have to dig the old codger up to find that magic key. Of course, it's always possible that he hid the wretched thing somewhere up at his house on Mount Creed. Isn't that a charming thought? We may have to go up to that dreary house and pry up floorboards and poke holes in walls! Oh, Lord above! I wish I had never heard of Evaristus Sloane or his filthy robot! And to think that I started the thing going when I stuck those eyes into its head. Oh, Roderick Childermass, you ought to send your brain out to the dry cleaner's!"

Tears came to Johnny's eyes. He hated to hear the professor blaming himself for something that wasn't his fault. "You didn't know, professor!" he said, shaking his head sadly. "How could you have known?"

"I should have been more cautious," said the professor bitterly. "But all this is neither here nor there: we'd better get ourselves in gear, or that metal monster is going to cut a bloody swath through half of New England. Charley Coote is trying to find out where old Sloane is buried. In the meantime, I think we're going to have to grit our teeth and go up to Stark Corners once again. Are you ready to go up with me? You don't have to if you don't want to."

Fergie and Johnny looked at each other quickly.

"You can count me in, prof!" said Fergie, and he thumped his fist on the table.

"Me, too!" said Johnny loudly.

"Good for you!" said the professor, beaming. He patted the two boys on the shoulder. "I'll make up some reason why you two need another weekend vacation in the mountains, and with some luck we ought to be able to leave by tomorrow afternoon. In the meantime, we'd all better lock our doors and hope that that thing out there doesn't want to come back."

Johnny shuddered as he thought about Mrs. Tremblay. If the robot came to get them, what could they do to stop it? What could they possibly do?

CHAPTER NINE

On the following evening, Fergie, Johnny, and the professor were up in the mountains. It was dark and again it was pouring rain, and the three of them were standing around and staring at the maroon Pontiac, which was pulled off onto a muddy piece of ground near the road. The car had a flat tire that sagged like a collapsed pudding. With a jack handle clenched in his fist, the professor stood staring down at the tire in disbelief. He was wearing an old rubber rain poncho, and he was almost speechless with rage.

"I *hate* cars!" he snarled through clenched teeth. "If the people who run this country had any imagination, we'd be able to take buses anywhere at any time, so we could avoid ridiculous messes like this one!" He heaved a deep sigh and wiped rain off his face with his sleeve. "Oh, well!" he said wearily. "I guess I'd better stop crabbing and start jacking this miserable crate up."

"Do you know how to work a jack, professor?" asked Johnny timidly.

The professor turned and glared at him. "I most certainly do!" he said indignantly. "I changed the tire of an army truck while we were being shelled, during the battle of the Argonne Forest. Now stand back, please, and give me some room!"

With a lot of grumbling and cursing, the professor got busy. He had to work in the dark because he had forgotten to bring a flashlight. Carefully, he edged the jack in under the car. Then he stuck the handle into the socket and started pumping. Slowly the car rose . . . and then something bad happened. With a lurch, the car rolled forward and the jack fell over—the professor had forgotten to put the car in gear. Swearing violently, the old man hurled the jack handle out into the middle of the road. Then he stomped out to get it, but as he was walking back he stopped and stared at something. Holding his hand up to shield his glasses from the rain, the professor peered for a long time.

"John!" he called. "John! Byron! Do my eyes deceive me, or is there a light down the road there?"

Johnny and Fergie walked out to where the professor was. Sure enough, far down the road a blob of yellow light could be seen.

"How about that!" said the professor as he took off his

glasses and dried them with his handkerchief. "I thought this road was deserted, so I never even bothered to . . . but see here! We're wasting time! Let's hike on down there and see if we can get some help. I'd love to have a hot cup of coffee and a chance to dry out, and I imagine you two feel the same way. Come on!"

The professor put his glasses back on, and the three of them tramped down the road through the falling rain. As they got closer, they began to make out the shadowy outline of a building. Fergie had the best eyes of the three, and he said that it looked like a gas station.

"Great!" said the professor, and he began to walk faster. "Wonderful! Maybe I'll be able to get some cigarettes—had to throw away my Balkan Sobranies because they got all soggy."

At last they arrived, and it did turn out to be a gas station after all. There were two Esso pumps, and a little one-story building with a slate roof. On the front of the building was an oblong window with a pink neon GAS sign in it, and nailed up next to the door was a blue Ex-Lax thermometer. Kicking spurts of water into the air, the professor ran forward and jerked open the screen door. He pushed at the inside door, and a little bell tingled. The boys crowded in behind the professor, and now all three of them were standing in the little store. There was a small, glass-topped display case that held cigars and pipe tobacco and next to it, in a corner, was a scarred wooden chair with a cat curled up on its seat. Behind the counter were shelves full of canned food and a door that probably led to a back room, but the door stayed closed. Nobody came to answer the bell.

"Humph!" said the professor as he glanced discontentedly around. "Isn't that just the limit! The attendant leaves the light on and the door open, and just goes away. It's not the kind of evening for a long stroll in the woods, is it? Oh, well—he may have been called away by some emergency. Let's see if he turns up."

They waited. A small metal clock on a shelf ticked noisily, and rain rattled on the roof. The cat slept peacefully. Finally, just as the professor was getting ready to go outside and search, the door behind the counter opened. Out stepped a tall, gaunt old man who wore grease-stained overalls and a blue work shirt. He had a big mop of white hair, and there was a wart the size of a pea near the end of his nose. The skin of the old man's face was saggy, and his eyes were red-rimmed. He looked as if he had been sick for a long time, and he moved slowly. Oddly enough, his hands were long, pale, delicate, and soft-skinned—they didn't look like the hands of a man who spent his time fixing cars and pumping gas.

"I'm sorry to have kept you folks waiting," said the man as he pulled the door shut behind him. "I must have dozed off, so I didn't hear the bell. Is there anything I can help you with?"

Johnny's eyebrows rose. He had expected the man to use bad grammar the way his grampa did. But the man spoke clearly and precisely, with a faint trace of an English accent. It was strange.

The professor had also noticed the man's peculiar way of speaking, but his mind was on other things—he wanted to get his flat tire fixed so they could all be on their way. Harrumphing and coughing, he put on his best business-like manner and told the old man what their problem was. The man stood dead still while the professor talked, but he didn't seem to be paying much attention to what he was saying.

"Hm . . . hm . . ." he said at last, "you say you have a flat tire? Unfortunately, I can't do any heavy work—I hurt my back some time ago. But I have a young man who helps me sometimes. Let me see if I can locate him."

As the professor stood drumming his fingers impatiently on the counter, the old man pulled a telephone out of a cubbyhole in the wall and gave the operator a number. He muttered into the phone for a bit, and then hung up.

"He'll be coming very soon," the man announced. Then he smiled strangely and added, "He doesn't have very far to go to get here—I'm lucky I found him in. Would you all like some coffee while you're waiting?"

The three travelers all nodded eagerly, and the old man disappeared into the back room again. Humming tune-lessly, the professor went to the window and watched the rain fall. Fergie took his jackknife out of his pocket, opened the small blade, and began cleaning his fingernails. Johnny started acting fidgety. He was getting more and more nervous by the minute, and he began to get the creepy idea that someone was staring at him. He could *feel* the stare—it was like heat coming from a radiator.

And the stare seemed to be coming from the row of shelves behind the counter. But when Johnny looked, he saw nothing but cans and boxes. He told himself that he was having his "emergency" jitters—every time something went wrong, he started imagining all sorts of wild things. So he paced and tried to ignore his feelings.

After about a quarter of an hour had passed, the old man came back with a tray and three china mugs full of hot coffee. Sighing wearily, he began handing the mugs around—one for the professor, one for Fergie, and one for Johnny. The coffee tasted delicious. As they sipped, the old man went to the door and peered out into the rainy darkness.

"Here he comes!" he said suddenly. "Ah! Good! He'll be able to help you. He'll have that flat fixed for you in no time!"

The professor peered out the door, and he saw a shadowy figure standing just outside the light. He wondered why he hadn't heard a car motor, but then it occurred to him that there were houses in the hills around this place. The young man had probably come down some mountain path, on foot. Oh, well, he was here—that was the important thing! Quickly the professor took another sip of coffee, but when he turned to Johnny, he stopped short. Johnny's face was deathly pale.

"I . . . I feel sick," he moaned. "I feel like I'm . . . coming down with somethin'. I'm sorry, I really am."

The professor sighed and patted Johnny on the shoulder. "John," he said, "you do not need to apologize for being ill. If you're sick, you're sick, as my dear mother used to say. Why don't you stay here and keep dry while we follow the mechanic back to the car? There's no reason for you to get soaked and catch pneumonia."

"The prof's right, John baby," Fergie added. "You stay here an' we'll be back in a jiffy. Okay?"

Johnny nodded. He was really miserable—he felt feverish and drowsy, and all the strength seemed to be draining out of his body. "All . . . all right," he muttered, rubbing his hand over his face. "I'll . . . see you guys . . . later."

Fergie and the professor went out, and the screen door slammed behind them. Johnny heard their footsteps as they splashed across the wet pavement. He couldn't understand why, but he felt vaguely frightened—he did not want to be left alone with the old man. *I'm just imagining things*, Johnny told himself. *You get weird ideas when you have a fever*. He turned and looked for someplace where he could sit down. But the cat was still sleeping in the chair, and the old man had not offered to find Johnny another seat. The clock ticked, and the rain pattered on. As Johnny watched blearily, the old man shuffled around the counter and started fussing with some cans that were on a shelf. With his back to Johnny, the man started to talk.

"Isn't it odd how you sometimes think someone is looking at you, when you're alone in a room?" he said suddenly.

Johnny's vision was blurring, and he was getting sleepier by the minute. But the words that the old man spoke struck terror into his heart. In a flash he was wide awake.

As he watched in horror, the man stepped to one side, and Johnny saw something on the shelf that he hadn't seen before. It was a yellowish human skull with two glass eyes in the hollow sockets. The old man grinned wickedly, and the skull stared, and the room whirled around Johnny. Then everything went black, and he fell unconscious to the floor.

CHAPTER TEN

The wind began to blow, and the rain swept by in sheets. With their backs bent, and arms raised to ward off the wet, Fergie and the professor followed the silent young man down the road. They hadn't seen the man's face yet— he was just a shadow moving in front of them while the faint beam of his flashlight played over the glistening pavement. Finally they reached the car, and the professor started hunting around in the mud to see where he had left the jack handle. Suddenly Fergie spoke.

"Hey, prof! What happened to the guy with the flashlight?"

The professor straightened up, and he looked around. He couldn't see much, but the flashlight beam had disappeared.

"Hey!" yelled the professor. "Hey! Turn the blasted light on again, will you? Hello? Where are you?"

Silence. With a loud curse, the professor stumbled toward the car, opened the passenger-side door, and groped in the glove compartment. He pulled out his Nimrod pipe lighter and lit it. A Nimrod lighter is shaped like a tube and works in stormy weather, but it doesn't give much light. With the flaming tube in his hand, the professor walked all the way around the car. On the other side he met Fergie, who was standing dead still with his arms folded.

"What do you think happened to that creep?" asked Fergie angrily. "Where did he go?"

The professor was beginning to get alarmed: he thought about the old man's strange accent, and Johnny's sudden illness. Snapping the lighter shut, he reached out and grabbed Fergie's arm.

"Byron! Come on!" he said, excitedly. "We've got to get back to that gas station! Quick!"

Fergie and the professor ran back along the wet road as fast as they could. They were getting thoroughly soaked, and their shoes squished, but they didn't care—they were in a state of total panic. When they got to the gas station, they saw it was dark and deserted. The light over the gas pumps had been turned out, and rain dripped from the hand-painted cardboard sign that hung from the doorknob—the sign said CLOSED.

With a violent yell, the professor jerked open the screen door. He raised his foot and kicked at the inner door—

once, twice, three times. The third kick did it, and the door swayed inward. Once again, the professor lit his lighter, and he looked around. The cat was gone, and the cans on the shelves behind the counter had been rearranged. Rushing forward, the professor kicked open the door behind the counter. There was nothing in the back room but darkness and a musty, shut-up smell. With a long, shuddering sigh, the professor snapped his lighter shut. He stumbled back out to the front room of the gas station and pounded his fists on the counter.

"Oh, what a *fool* I was!" he exclaimed. "What an unbelievable addlepated fool! I should have realized that something was wrong, and I should never have left John here alone! This mess is all my fault! If I hadn't dreamed up that wild, harebrained plan to find Sloane's robot and strike out Cliff Bullard, John would be home in his bed, safe and sound! This is terrible! What on *earth* are we going to do?"

As Fergie watched, the professor broke down. He put his face in his hands and sobbed. Finally, when he was all cried out, he pulled out his soggy handkerchief and blew his nose loudly. But as he was stuffing his handkerchief into his pocket, he let out a loud exclamation.

Fergie jumped. "Hey! Hey, what is it, prof? Did you remember somethin'?"

The professor gritted his teeth. "Yes, I remembered something!" he growled. "A long time ago, Henry Dixon told me that Evaristus Sloane had a large wart near the end of his nose. Byron, that old man was *Evaristus Sloane*!"

Fergie's jaw dropped. "*Huh?* I thought you said he was dead."

The professor bit his lip. "That was another mistake that I made. Sloane was about thirty years old when he made the robot that we found, and that was fifty-three years ago, so he's in his eighties now. Charley Coote and I had figured he was dead, but we figured wrong. Oh, what fools we were! No wonder poor Charley couldn't find out where he was buried! Sloane is alive! And he's still practicing the black arts. That 'young man' was just a spectre that he raised up to lead us away from here while he kidnaped John! I can't imagine why he wanted to take him, but if we don't find the two of them in a hurry . . . well, I don't like to think about what might happen."

Fergie clenched his fists. "If I catch that old creep, I'll tie his magic wand in a knot and stick it in his ear!" he said hatefully.

"Atta boy!" said the professor, patting Fergie on the arm. "We'll fix the rotten swine! First, however, we've got to find him, and that may be rather difficult. Where do you think we ought to look? Have you got any bright ideas?"

Fergie rubbed his chin. "I think we oughta go up to the house in the mountains, just like we were gonna do before we had our flat tire. Maybe they won't be there, but it's as good a place as any to try."

The professor nodded. "I think you're right—it's the only thing we can do. But before we do anything, we are going to have to go back and change that rotten flat tire. I feel tired, but I think I can do it with your help. How does it look outside?"

Fergie opened the door and poked his head out. The rain was letting up, and overhead he could see a ghostly moon behind racing clouds.

"I think the rain's gonna stop, prof," he said. "It won't be so bad out there now—just kinda muddy. I bet we can get the tire changed."

The professor heaved a deep sigh and wiped rain off his poncho with his hand. "It'll have to be done, I suppose," he said wearily. "If I had stuck with the job and finished it, we wouldn't be in this mess—but there's no use crying over spilled milk. Come on, my stouthearted friend. Off we go!"

While Fergie and the professor struggled to change the tire, Johnny lay on the back seat of a car that bounced and jounced over a rugged mountain road. He kept waking up and blacking out, over and over again, and whenever he tried to move his arms and legs, he found that he couldn't. Finally the car jolted to a stop. Johnny heard a car door slam, and then the door near his head opened, and he was roughly dragged out onto the ground. Standing over him was the tall, stooped old man, the gas station owner.

"So nice to meet you!" said the man as he grabbed Johnny by the collar and started dragging him across the wet grass. "You're Henry Dixon's grandson, aren't you?

I thought I would have to go down to Duston Heights to get you, but you came up here to me! How very convenient! You know, your grandfather did me wrong many years ago, and now I'm going to get even. And you're going to help me. Don't you feel honored? Of *course* you do! I *knew* you'd be pleased! Wait till you see what I've made. It's almost done, but it needs a few finishing touches, if you know what I mean. Years ago, I made a mechanical man that worked because its eyes were really the eyes of a living human being—a human who had been living at one time, that is. I used an ancient magic formula to do this, and I added a little extra twist of my own. For a long time I had been fascinated by the legend that says that a dead man's eyes reflect the last thing he ever saw on earth. But what if the last thing he sees is *himself*? When I killed that poor man to make my robot, I held a mirror up to his face, and then, later, when I put his eyes in the robot, it took on the shape of a *real human being!* That is, it took on the shape of the man I had killed. Imagine how pleased I felt when I knew that I had improved on the old formula!" The old man paused and sighed. "Unfortunately," he went on, "the robot didn't work out, but you are going to help me remedy that. You are going to contribute to a great scientific experiment. Doesn't that make you feel proud?"

Johnny only heard about half of what the old man was saying. His body felt numb, and his mind kept drifting off into a dreamy world where nothing mattered at all. He was terribly frightened, but when he tried to speak, his lips wouldn't move. Meanwhile, the old man tugged at his collar, and Johnny's limp body bumped over the rough ground. The old man was whistling softly, but just as Johnny was wondering what tune it was, he blacked out again.

Later, Johnny awoke. He was lying on a hard surface, and everything around him looked blurry. Where were his glasses? The old man must have taken them off, or maybe they had fallen off when he was being dragged across the ground. Where was he now? Vague shapes swam before his eyes. Then he heard someone cough, and he saw shadowy hands moving near him. The old man was slipping Johnny's glasses onto his head, and now he was propping him up so he could see. Warily, Johnny looked around: he was in a room with rough stone walls, and he was lying on a table. Near him, on a marble-topped washstand, glittering instruments—a scalpel, a probe—lay in a row. Next to the instruments lay a small hand mirror, and nearby stood a large glass jar that was half full of dark green moss. Against one wall of the room an old oak sideboard loomed, and three oil lamps burned on top of it. Near the lamps stood a bronze incense burner, and bluish smoke curled up from the holes in its lid. At the far end of the room stood something large—a statue, maybe— that was draped with a painter's drop cloth. The old man started to speak.

"So here we are. Isn't this a nice place?" he crooned in a threatening voice. "I hope you're comfortable, but if you aren't, I'm afraid there's not much you can do about it. The drug that I put in your coffee will keep you paralyzed for quite some time. Unfortunately, it doesn't keep you from feeling pain, but then, we can't have everything, can we? Now before we begin, I wonder if you'd care to see my new creation. I'll have to wait forty days before it can be used, but I'm a patient man. Alas, this will be your only chance to see it, so make the most of your opportunity. Are you ready?"

Johnny's head was lowered back onto the hard table, and he heard footsteps moving down to the other end of the room. There was a swishing sound, and then the footsteps returned. The old man propped Johnny's head up again, and he saw the thing that had been hidden by the drop cloth. His heart began to hammer hard, and a soundless scream burst inside his head. There on a stone pedestal stood a gaunt figure made of shining metal. It was shaped to look like a shriveled corpse with spindly arms and legs. The head was like a skull covered with glittering skin, and the large hollow eye sockets were empty.

CHAPTER ELEVEN

Once again, the maroon Pontiac was bumping along the rutty road that led up the side of Mount Creed. The professor gripped the steering wheel hard, and he cursed every time the car hit a bump. Fergie sat beside him, and the look on his face showed that he was frightened but determined. They were going much too fast on this winding road, and sometimes the car skidded very close to the edge when the professor rounded a curve. But Fergie didn't complain—he knew they were in a desperate hurry, and he only hoped that they were going in the right direction. After they had careened round a tight hairpin turn, the professor began to slow down. Up ahead of them a car was parked in the middle of the road.

"Hah!" said the professor as he put on the brakes and

turned off the engine. "I'll bet you that's old Sloane's car. Who else would be up on this godforsaken mountain at this time of night? Well, that proves that we've come to the right place. And in case there was any doubt in your mind, it also proves that Sloane is no ghost—ghosts don't need cars to take them from one place to the next. All right! Everybody out! We're going the rest of the way on foot!"

Fergie and the professor got out, and they edged past the old rusty Chevrolet, moving quickly. The clouds had cleared and the moon was out, and this helped them see where they were going. The road had stopped winding, and climbed straight up the side of the mountain. Dark masses of bushes and trees loomed on both sides.

"I . . . I wish I had brought a weapon of . . . some kind," the professor gasped as he paused to catch his breath. "The jack handle—we might have been able to use it."

"It's a heck of a time to be thinkin' about that," grumbled Fergie as he wiped his forehead with his sleeve. "By the way, do you think we're gettin' close? It's hard to tell in the dark."

The professor squinted into the gloom. "I can't be positively sure, but I think the house is around that curve up there—you see it, way up ahead?"

Fergie nodded. "I guess so. Okay, I've got my wind back, so let's get movin'. You all right?"

The professor grinned. "Except for nervous prostration, exhaustion, and a fierce ache in my side, I'm in great shape!" he said. "Forward, at the gallop!"

Fergie and the professor started to run. They both had the feeling that something awful was going to happen to Johnny, and they wanted to get to the house as fast as they possibly could. As they drew closer to the curve in the road, they saw that the professor had been right: there was the grassy field glimmering in the moonlight, and in the distance the shadowy house waited. But there was something standing in the field, near the edge of the road. A post? No. It was someone with a rifle in his hands.

Fergie and the professor stopped running. Cold fear swept over them, and they glanced quickly at each other. With crunching sounds, the figure moved closer, and now they could see that it was a teenager, a boy who was maybe fifteen years old. He had a pimply face and a crew cut, and he looked mean.

"Okay, you two!" he yelled. "That's as far as you go! Back off!"

The professor clenched his fists. He could feel anger welling up inside him. With an effort, he managed to keep calm. "Young man," he said in a strained voice, "you must have a lot of spare time on your hands. I mean, here you are, with a gun in your hands, guarding a deserted empty house. May I ask why?"

"House isn't deserted," snapped the boy, and he waved the rifle around to show that he meant business. "It belongs to Mr. Oglesby, an' he pays me t'look after the place. He called me up from his gas station, an' he said fer me t'come up here 'bout ten o'clock an' keep people away. An' I do what he tells me to do. So get movin', er you'll be sorry."

Fergie turned to the professor. "Who's Oglesby?" he whispered.

"That must be the name Sloane is using," the professor muttered. And he added nastily, "I'd like to wring that kid's neck! He thinks he's the king of the hill with that wretched piece of artillery in his hands!"

"Huh? What'd you say?" asked the boy in a threatening voice.

"None o' your business," snapped Fergie.

There was silence for about a minute. The boy stood tensely gripping the rifle in his hands, while Fergie and the professor stood several paces away, watching him. Finally Fergie stepped forward. He looked the boy up and down contemptuously, and folded his arms.

"Okay, you!" he said loudly. "Are you *really* gonna shoot us if we try to get past you? Are you that dumb? You shoot us, an' you'll get tossed in jail fer the rest o' your life! How'd you like fer *that* to happen? Huh?"

The boy stiffened. "Who're you callin' dumb, you long-nosed goop? You say that to me again, an' I'll push your face in!"

"You an' who else?" said Fergie in a taunting voice. "I bet you couldn't fight yer way out of a paper bag!"

As the professor watched in amazement, the boy threw down his rifle and rushed at Fergie. Swearing, he lunged at Fergie's throat, but Fergie ducked to one side and landed a punch in the boy's stomach. They started rolling around in the grass, kicking and snarling. Quickly the professor sprang forward. He picked up the rifle, slid the bolt back, and dumped the bullet out. Then he threw the rifle down and tried to break up the fight. The pimply-faced kid had a cut lip and some red marks on his face.

"Had enough?" snarled Fergie. He raised his right fist in the air threateningly.

"All right, you two!" barked the professor. "The fight's over. There are more important things to be attended to! Break it up!" He bent over and grabbed Fergie by the shoulders, but at that moment something happened. From the underbrush across the road came a loud crackling and crunching. Boughs swayed and bent, and suddenly a large, man-sized shape lurched out into the middle of the road.

In an instant, the professor guessed. "Oh, my God!" he gasped. "It's the robot!"

Swaying uncertainly, the thing looked around. In the moonlight it was hard to tell, but it looked like a big husky man with a shock of blond hair on his head. The robot had taken on the shape that it had when it struck out Clutch Klemm in the summer of 1900.

"Run, everybody, *run!*" yelled the professor in a panicky voice. "That thing isn't human, and if it catches you, it'll kill you! For God's sake, let's *go!* Come on, while we have the chance!"

Nobody needed to be warned a second time. Before the professor had finished speaking, the pimply-faced boy took off on the dead run across the field. Fergie and the professor galloped toward the house, and the crunching sounds they heard behind them made them run even harder. They didn't stop until they were standing on the shadowy front porch of the house.

"Is . . . is it . . . coming . . . after us?" gasped the professor. He was holding his side and wincing with pain.

Fergie looked. The hulking moonlit figure was plodding along at a steady pace through the tall grass. Apparently the robot did not believe in hurrying.

As soon as he had caught his breath, the professor dashed into the house, with Fergie right behind him. The rooms were empty and dark, and there was no sound. Sudden despair filled the professor's heart—had they come to the wrong place? Then, as he was struggling to fight back tears, he heard it. A small sound, a distant clinking and clattering. It seemed to be coming from down below, in the basement.

"*Come on!*" yelled the professor as he grabbed Fergie's arm. "We've got to find the kitchen! I mean, the cellar door! Follow me!"

They stumbled down a dark hallway, bumping into doors on the way. In the distance, moonlight was shining on a worn linoleum floor, and that guided them. Once they had reached the kitchen, Fergie and the professor began looking wildly around. One door opened into a closet, and another led to the pantry. Where was the door that led to the basement? Then, as he paused in the middle of the room, the professor looked down. A linoleum-covered door lay at his feet. With a yell he dropped to his knees and grabbed the little ring that served as a door-knob. Pulling the heavy door back, the professor peered down into the blackness. He could just barely make out a rickety flight of steps. Carefully he began to pick his way down, and Fergie followed.

The basement smelled musty and damp, and it was absolutely pitch dark—except for one thing. A tiny, pencil-thin line of light could be seen over in one corner. Groping his way forward, the professor found that he was standing in front of a set of wooden shelves that was full of Mason jars. The light was coming from a crack in a wooden door that stood behind the shelves. Furiously the professor hurled jars this way and that, and the basement was filled with the sound of breaking glass. With Fergie's help, he heaved the shelves sideways and kicked open the door.

Fergie and the professor stopped in the doorway, and they stared. Before them lay a rock-walled room that was lit by three oil lamps. On a table lay Johnny, stiff and still and deathly pale, and near him stood the old man from the gas station. He was wearing a white smock and rubber gloves, and in one hand he held a glittering sharp scalpel. The other hand clutched a mirror.

"*You dirty dog!*" screeched the professor, and he rushed at the man, knocking him backwards across the marble-topped stand. Instruments clattered to the floor, and the glass jar full of moss shattered. The old man fell, but he sprang up nimbly with the scalpel still in his hand. He lunged at the professor, but he missed, and suddenly the professor was on him, hammering at his midsection and yelling all sorts of unpleasant things. The old man crumpled. The professor's foot came down on his wrist, and the scalpel fell from his fingers.

"*There!*" snarled the professor fiercely. His face was beet red, and he was breathing hard. "You rotten fourteenth-rate excuse for a human being!" he roared. "I'll fix you, by the eternal powers I will!"

The old man lay on the floor, cowering. "Please . . . please don't kill me," he said in a quavering voice.

The professor glanced down, and then he turned away. Fergie was standing by the table, his hand on Johnny's heart. With fear in his eyes, he looked up.

"He's alive, prof!" said Fergie. "I mean, his heart's beatin', but he's out cold. Whaddaya think that old crud did to him?"

"He probably fainted from sheer terror," snapped the professor. "And he may be drugged. Can you lift him? We'll just have to try to . . ."

The professor's voice died away. From the dark basement that lay beyond the doorway came the sound of crunching glass. Heavy footsteps moved closer, and then the robot came lurching into the lamplit room. Its large blue eyes were lit by an evil, insane glow. As soon as he saw the thing, the old man let out a bloodcurdling yell and scrambled to his feet. He stood cowering against the wall, and he covered his face with his hands.

"Oh, my Lord, no!" he sobbed. "No, no! What have you fools done? What have you *done*?"

CHAPTER TWELVE

A hush fell over the room. Fergie stood watching the robot, with Johnny's head propped up in his hands. The professor's mind was racing—he was trying to remember the name of the thing that you were supposed to use to control the robot. And then it came to him.

"The *key*!" he exclaimed, turning to the old man. "Sloane, you detestable wretch! Where is the Key of Arbaces? Do you have it?"

Sloane took his hands away from his face. "It . . . it's in the sideboard behind you. In the top drawer. It—"

Suddenly the robot moved forward. With heavy, dragging steps, it stumped past the table where Johnny lay and reached out its arms to grab Sloane. He shrieked and dodged out of the way, and the robot bumped clumsily against the wall. Meanwhile, the professor was fumbling madly with pot holders and medicine bottles in the top drawer of the sideboard. Finally the professor's fingers closed over a key. It looked like an ordinary house key, and a cardboard tag dangled from it on a string.

"Is this it? Is this the key?" he yelled waving the key in the air.

"Yes! Yes!" Sloane babbled as he moved farther along the wall. "Put it in the hole in the back of his neck and turn it! For God's sake, *hurry*!"

As Sloane talked, the robot began shuffling along next to the wall like a great oversized toy. Then it took three steps toward Sloane and, with a sweep of its arm, knocked him to his knees. With the key in his hand, the professor began to sneak up behind the robot. He was horribly afraid that the thing would turn on him, but it was not interested in anyone but Evaristus Sloane. Seizing Sloane by the shoulders, the robot picked him up and slammed him against the wall. The professor crept closer, and now he could see a small oblong hole in the creature's neck. It was just above his shirt collar. With a sudden leap, the professor reached up, plunged the key into the hole, and twisted it. The robot stiffened, and its arms fell to its sides. It turned halfway round, and then fell to the floor with a loud metallic clatter. The professor and Fergie looked down, and as they watched, the robot's body shimmered and wavered. The human form melted away, and there lay the shiny aluminum man in his metal base- ball uniform.

As the professor was trying to figure out what to do next, Sloane made a dash for the door.

"Hey!" Fergie yelled. "Go after him, prof! Are you gonna let that rat get away?"

"He can run all the way to the St. Lawrence Seaway, for all I care!" growled the professor. "We'd better get Johnny back to the car. Maybe we can find a doctor in Stark Corners who will be willing to look him over. Let's get a move on!"

Quickly the professor glanced at the corpselike metal statue that stood in a corner of the room. He shuddered, and then he moved to the end of the table and lifted Johnny's legs. Fergie put his hands under Johnny's armpits, and together they carried him out of the room and across the dark basement. As they maneuvered Johnny up the cellar steps, the professor half expected to see Evaristus Sloane waiting for them with a pistol or an axe in his hands. Fortunately, though, he wasn't there, and they went on their way with Johnny's limp body, out the back door of the house and across the field toward the road. Johnny began to groan and make muffled noises. He tossed his head like somebody having a bad dream.

"Thank God!" breathed the professor. "The way he looked, I thought he was three quarters of the way toward death. Hang on, my boy—hang on! We're going to get help for you as soon as we can!"

A little while later, the professor and Fergie were sitting in the waiting room of a doctor's office. They had taken Johnny to the first doctor they could find, a Dr.

Smethers who lived in a large Victorian house on the main street of Stark Corners. The doctor had been a bit annoyed when Fergie and the professor banged on his door late at night, but as soon as he saw that there was a real emergency, he got to work. He had been examining Johnny for a long time, and Fergie and the professor were starting to get impatient. The longer they waited, the more they worried about Johnny. Maybe he was dying, and the doctor was afraid to tell them. Whatever the situation was, they wanted to know about it.

Finally Dr. Smethers opened the door. He was a very distinguished-looking man with a gray mustache and curly hair.

"Well?" said the professor as he jumped up out of his seat.

The doctor smiled reassuringly. "Relax," he said. "Your friend is going to be all right. He was given some drug that I don't know the name of—a muscle-relaxing drug like curare. At any rate, he didn't get a big dose, and the effects are starting to wear off. What on earth happened to the poor boy?"

The professor looked the doctor straight in the eye. He tried hard to seem sincere and honest. "He was grabbed by a madman who had set up some sort of insane laboratory in the basement of an old stone house up on Mount Creed. We were camped near there, and we managed to get Johnny away from this character. But he may still be up there. Will you call the police to the house to see if they can nab him?"

The doctor looked grave. "I certainly will!" he said in a shocked voice. "Good Lord, that's the old Sloane place! It has certainly seen its share of evil goings-on over the years—but then, that's something you wouldn't know about, would you? Look, I'll go call the police and see how your friend is doing. Stay calm—everything's going to be all right!"

The professor and Fergie settled down in a couple of easy chairs and started going through a tall stack of *National Geographic*s. After half an hour, two policemen arrived, and they looked pretty upset. According to them, the Sloane house had been on fire when they arrived on the scene. It was burning like a torch, and since there was no source of water nearby, they couldn't do anything but watch it.

"Good Lord!" exclaimed the professor. "So the old place is gone! I'll bet one of those oil lamps got upset—we saw three of them in the basement of the house when we . . . but see here, gentlemen! Dr. Smethers must have told you on the phone about the things that happened to us up at that house."

"He told us somethin'," said the taller policeman as he reached into his shirt pocket for a pen and a pad of paper. "But we'd like to get some kind of statement from you. Are you ready to give us one?"

The professor sighed unhappily. He knew that he would have to tell the two cops the same story that he had told Dr. Smethers. Once again he recited his odd little half-true tale, but this time he gave a very exact description of

Evaristus Sloane. When he got to the part about the wart on Sloane's nose, the tall cop let out a loud exclamation.

"My gosh!" he said. "That's old Emmett Oglesby, the guy that runs the gas station out on the highway! I always thought he was a nice old fella, the kind that wouldn't hurt a fly!"

"Well, you never know about some people," said the professor, his jaw clenched. "If you can catch the old creep, I think he ought to be charged with kidnaping and maybe attempted murder, or at least assault with intent to do great bodily harm."

The tall cop gave the professor a dirty look—he hated it when people threw legal terms at him. "We'll do what we can, sir," he said coldly. "But in the meantime I wanta ask you: Do you have any idea why Mr. Oglesby would want to kidnap this kid?"

The professor shook his head. "I haven't the foggiest idea, officer," he said. "If you can see into the mind of a vicious lunatic, you are a lot cleverer than I am. If you find out anything, I have left my name and telephone number with Dr. Smethers. For now, I think I will be happy when I find out that young John Dixon is well enough to go back to Duston Heights with me."

The policemen left, and Dr. Smethers came out of his office and announced that Johnny was ready to go. "He'll probably sleep on the way home," he explained as he led Fergie and the professor into the inner office. "By the way, are you sure you wouldn't rather spend the night up here at the inn? It's pretty late."

The professor shook his head. "No. I'd rather drive straight home. I'm wide awake, and if I can get a cup of strong tea from you, I'll make it all right."

Dr. Smethers boiled some water on the hot plate in his office, and the professor had tea. Meanwhile Fergie talked to Johnny, who was pale and woozy, but otherwise cheerful. The professor paid the doctor, thanked him, and left with the boys. Johnny got into the backseat of the Pontiac, stretched out, and fell asleep immediately. Fergie and the professor climbed into the front seat, and they drove off. To Fergie's surprise, the professor did not head toward U.S. 302, which would have taken them home. Instead he went the other way, on the road that led toward Mount Creed.

"What are you up to, prof?" asked Fergie, who was beginning to get alarmed. "Aren't we supposed to be headin' home?"

"We *will* be heading home—eventually," said the professor as he swerved off onto the mountain road. "But I will not be able to rest until I find out if Sloane rescued his two robots and the magic key before he torched the house. You don't have to come along. In fact, I want you to stay in the car with John until I return. I won't be gone long, so don't worry."

The professor drove up the road. They passed Sloane's car, which had been shoved off into a deep ditch by the policemen, and kept going until they reached the place where the road became impossibly bumpy and rocky. The professor got out, and Fergie heard the trunk lid slam.

By the light of the setting moon, he saw the professor stalk up the road with the jack handle clutched firmly in his fist. Time passed. After half an hour the professor returned. His hands and face were smudged with soot, there were burn holes on his shirt and trousers, and he was scowling hatefully.

"Didja find out anything?" asked Fergie as the professor climbed into the driver's seat.

Angrily the professor slammed the car door and shoved the jack handle into Fergie's hands. "Do I *look* as if I found out anything?" he snapped. "*No!* The house is still smoldering, and all the timbers and some of the stone walls have fallen into the basement. The place is still glowing like a blast furnace. Maybe we can come up here again in a few days after the fire has burned itself out." And with that, he shoved the key into the ignition and started the car.

As the professor was turning the car around, Fergie glanced at Johnny, who was still sound asleep in the backseat. Then he peered out the window at the dark mountain that loomed above them. "It's too bad you couldn't get into the old dump," he muttered glumly. "But look, prof—are you sure you can drive all the way home without fallin' asleep at the wheel? It's a pretty long way to go."

"Oh, I'll be all right," said the professor, shrugging. "But I would like to ask a favor of you: Would you sing *Ninety-Eight Bottles of Beer on the Wall*? You know, the song the Boy Scouts sing on long bus rides?"

Fergie laughed. "Yeah, sure—I'll sing it. But would you mind my askin' why?"

"Not at all," said the professor. "It's a song I hate, and if I'm annoyed, I'll stay awake till we get home. Any more questions? No? Then start singing. We've got a long way to go!"

CHAPTER THIRTEEN

They got back to Duston Heights in the wee small hours of the morning. It was much too late to be waking up the Dixons and the Fergusons, so the professor put the boys up at his house. Fergie was very tired and went upstairs and fell asleep immediately. But Johnny was wide awake now, and the professor was still running on nervous energy, so the two of them sat in the kitchen and talked for a while. Johnny had guessed that the old man was Evaristus Sloane, and he had a pretty good idea of what Sloane had intended to do to him. The horror of the experience was still fresh in his mind, and every now and then he would pause, close his eyes, and shudder.

"But how could he still be alive, professor?" Johnny asked, as he sipped the cocoa the professor had made.

"Didn't you say that he had died?"

The professor looked uncomfortable. "That's what I thought," he said with a sigh. "Which shows that you should never jump to conclusions. He's alive, and from what you told me, he's still sore at your grandfather because he made the Spiders turn down the baseball-pitching robot. He was going to use you to get even with Henry."

"That's crazy!" Johnny exclaimed. "I mean, how could anybody carry a grudge for—"

"For fifty years?" said the professor, with a wry smile. "A crazy person could, and Sloane is as batty as they come. If you want any further evidence that he's crazy, consider this: He's trying to make another robot like the original one!"

Johnny thought about this as he drank more cocoa. "Do . . . do you think he knew that we had found his old robot and put it together?" he asked hesitantly.

The professor shook his head. "No. Oddly enough, I think he wanted it left where he had hidden it fifty years before. He must have gotten to dislike it for some reason. Maybe that's why he dismantled it. He seemed very surprised when the evil creature came stumping into his laboratory, and he wouldn't have reacted that way if he had known we had found the robot." The professor paused and bit his lip. He raised his fist and brought it down on the table with a bang. "Lord!" he exclaimed. "I wish I knew what happened to him! I'd like to think that he wandered off into the woods and died, but that would just be wishful thinking. He won't dare go back to that gas station, but he just might come down here to Duston Heights. If you see any sign of the old devil, let me know immediately. You will do that, won't you, John?"

Johnny agreed, and after they talked for a while longer, he stumbled upstairs to the spare bedroom that the professor had fixed up for him. Johnny, Fergie, and the professor all slept until noon the next day. After a leisurely brunch, they went across the street to tell Gramma and Grampa what had happened. The professor did not want to upset the old people, so he told them the story that he had told the policemen in Stark Corners. The Dixons were very shocked. They thought that they lived in a peaceful corner of New England, and to have this happen right after the Tremblay break-in—well, it was all pretty hard for them to believe. When the professor took Fergie home and told the Fergusons the story, they were pretty upset too, and they wondered what the world was coming to.

Days passed, and September slid into October. The Stark Corners police called Johnny up to question him, and they said that Emmett Oglesby hadn't been captured yet. The New Hampshire newspapers had a field day with the story of the gas station madman, but they lost interest quickly when the police were unable to find Oglesby. The professor kept checking in the papers for additional information, and one evening, without telling anyone, he made a quick trip up to Stark Corners to see if he could do a little archeology in the ruins of Sloane's old house. But when he arrived, he found that the bulldozers had gotten there ahead of him. There was nothing left but a flat patch of raw earth littered with chunks of broken stone and pieces of window glass. The professor tried to feel relieved: he told himself that the two robots and the Key of Arbaces were buried under a lot of rubble, buried for good. But he really didn't know that for sure, and his doubts tormented him. He kept having the awful feeling that something more was going to happen.

Johnny was still pretty nervous too. The terror of his dreadful experience had not completely worn off, and he often dreamed that he was still a prisoner in Sloane's lamp-lit basement chamber. Once he had a particularly horrible dream in which he imagined that he was following his grandfather down Merrimack Street in the middle of the night. The old man turned into one of the narrow alleys that led down to the river, and Johnny saw a thing take shape at the far end of the alley. It was a monstrous bulging eye, lit by a trembling pale light. As Johnny watched in horror, his grandfather walked straight toward the eye and was swallowed up by it. He melted into the jellyish thing and vanished, while Johnny screamed and screamed.

But as the early days of October slid by, Johnny calmed down a bit. He began to notice signs throughout the city that proudly announced that the New York Yankee slugger, Cliff Bullard, would be at Duston Heights Athletic Stadium on October the fifteenth to offer ten thousand dollars to any local hurler who could strike him out. Fergie and Johnny spent a lot of time discussing the strikeout contest. They decided that none of the pitchers on the Duston Heights High School baseball team could blow three quick ones past Bullard. Maybe some kid from Andover or Merrimac or Newburyport would show up and amaze the world with his blazing fastball, but it didn't seem likely. Cliff Bullard would probably get to keep his ten thousand smackers, at least for a little while longer. As for the professor, he was totally batty on the subject of Cliff Bullard: every time Johnny or Fergie brought Bullard's name up, the professor would start ranting and raving about what a blowhard and emptyhead the man was. Finally it got to the point where the boys simply didn't talk to the professor at all about the big Yankee left fielder.

Toward the end of the first week of October, the weather changed. A warm wind began to blow, and the days got hot and hazy. Temperatures climbed into the eighties, and people dug their summer clothes out of the closet. One day after school, Johnny decided that he would go out and read on the front porch, the way he usually did in the summer. So, with a glass of iced tea on the table near his elbow, he settled himself on the old creaky glider and started reading *Quo Vadis*, a novel about ancient Rome. But Johnny had not gotten a lot of sleep the night before, and he began to feel drowsy. He turned a page, sipped some tea, and felt his eyes beginning to close. With a sigh, he took off his glasses, folded them neatly, and laid them on the table next to the iced tea glass. He took off his shoes, stretched out on the glider, and put a soiled green- and yellow-striped pillow under his head. *Buzz . . . buzz . . . buzz . . .* a fly was bumping against the screen, and its soft drone lulled him to sleep.

Nothing disturbed Johnny's contented breathing, and he did not hear someone pad softly up the porch steps, open the screen door, and step in. The person hovered over Johnny, watching him sleep. It was an old man, an old man with white hair and red-rimmed eyes and a wart near the end of his long, pointed nose. The man picked up Johnny's glasses, and from his pocket he took a small, cobalt-blue glass vial. Pulling the tiny cork from the bottle's mouth, the man dabbed a clear fluid on the lenses of the glasses, and his lips began to move as if he were muttering a prayer. Finally he laid the glasses back down on the table, and after a quick scornful glance at the sleeping boy, he turned and walked quietly away.

When Johnny woke up a few minutes later, he had the odd feeling that something was wrong. He sat up, shook his head woozily, and reached for his glasses. Suddenly he stopped. His glasses had been moved! Johnny was very fussy about his personal belongings, and he always remembered exactly where he had put his glasses. In this case, he had laid them on the doily next to the iced tea glass. But now they were on the bare tabletop, several inches away from the doily. With an irritated frown, he put the glasses on, got up, and walked into the house. He went straight to the front parlor, where his grandmother was sitting on the sofa watching television.

"Gramma," he said in an accusing tone, "did you fool around with my glasses?" He thought that maybe she had lifted them when she was dusting the table.

Gramma looked up in a startled way. "Your glasses?

No, John, I most certainly did not touch your glasses. Why? What happened?"

"Well, *somebody* moved 'em," he said sullenly.

"Maybe you forgot where you laid 'em," said Gramma, chuckling. "Or maybe they got up on their little skinny legs an' scooted away."

Johnny glowered. He might have known that his grandmother would think the whole thing was a joke—she was always kidding him about his fussbudgety ways. He was beginning to feel like an idiot, and he wondered if he had made a mistake. Maybe he really had laid the glasses down in the place where he found them. He shrugged and went out to the kitchen to get a glass of milk.

Days passed, and Johnny began to have trouble with his eyes. When he was reading in the evening, the page would start to blur in front of him, and he would feel dizzy. And sometimes when he was just walking along the street, he would feel that the sidewalk was rushing up to meet him. He got headaches during movies, and a lot of the time he felt nervous and edgy. Since he had poor eyesight, Johnny was afraid of going blind, and he often tormented himself with fears of what it would be like if the world around him was just a wall of blackness. For a while he kept his worries to himself, but finally he decided that he had to tell the professor. The professor had bad eyesight too, and he would be sympathetic if it turned out that Johnny had glaucoma or some other hideous eye disease. He would give Johnny a shoulder to cry on.

When Johnny at last got up the courage to talk to the professor, the old man was very sympathetic.

"Your eyes are just changing, John," the professor explained. "Everybody who's nearsighted has that problem. When I was about fifty my eyes started getting weaker, and I had to have different glasses. Do you know what I would suggest that you do?"

"What?"

"I would suggest that you go talk to your grandmother. She has been seeing a new optometrist, and she thinks the woman is wonderful. I forget her name, but she has an office downtown, in the First National Bank building. Go talk to your grandmother about her—I'm sure she'll give you all the information you need."

Johnny went to talk to Gramma later that day, and he found that she was very enthusiastic about the new optometrist, a lady named Dr. Pimlico. Gramma had just gotten a new set of glasses from her, and they were very comfortable and satisfactory in every way.

"An' she's cheap too," Gramma added. "She don't try t'soak you, the way old Dr. Liddy used to do. You'll feel a lot better once you get a new pair o'glasses from her."

So it was decided. Gramma called up Dr. Pimlico and made an appointment for Johnny on Friday, at two P.M. Friday afternoon, the professor offered to give Johnny a ride to the optometrist's office. As soon as Johnny got into the car, the professor noticed that he was very nervous. Johnny always got the heebie-jeebies whenever he went to a doctor of any kind, even one that wasn't going to hurt him. So the professor tried to cheer him up.

"I think you should relax, John," said the professor as they rolled along. "I'm sure that Dr. Pimlico is really quite an excellent eye doctor, and I wouldn't hesitate to go to her myself. By the way, that's an odd name, isn't it? Pimlico, I mean. It's the name of one of the sections of London: a long time ago, Londoners started giving names to the different parts of their city, names like Belgravia and Bayswater and Pimlico. But you know, I really haven't met a *person* named Pimlico before. And do you want to know something else that's interesting? Dr. Pimlico has a nephew who has entered the Bullard strikeout contest! I hear that he pitches for a high school team in Newington, and he has a real scorcher of a fastball. I hope he can manage to fog it past Bullard! Wouldn't it be funny if a high school pitcher from a burg like Newington struck out that overinflated balloon? I would laugh for *days* if that happened!"

The professor chattered merrily on, but Johnny really wasn't listening to him. He was getting more jittery by the minute, and he was racking his brain to see if he could find a way to get out of his appointment with the eye doctor. He couldn't remember ever being this edgy about an optometrist before, and he told himself that he was being silly—the doctor couldn't give him shots or operate on him. He was just going to get his eyes examined and maybe be fitted with a new set of glasses. That kind of thing was never painful, so why was he in such a bad state? Johnny thought that he was having some leftover fear from the awful experience he had had in Sloane's laboratory. *You're being a total nitwit*, he told himself. *Snap out of it.*

The professor's voice cut in on Johnny's thoughts. "Well, here you are, my lad!" he said as he pulled the car over to the curb. "I'm going to run down to a used bookstore at the other end of the street, and I'll be back to pick you up in about an hour. Please try to be less nitty— you'd think you were Sidney Carton marching off to the guillotine. Relax! It's the secret of having a long and healthy life!"

Johnny opened the car door and got out. He walked into the dark, cool bank building, got into an elevator, and pushed the button for the fifth floor. Up and up rose the car with a gentle humming sound. Finally it stopped, and the metal doors slid back. Johnny got out, mopped his forehead with his handkerchief, and started down the slippery tiled corridor. At last he came to a halt in front of a door with a frosted glass pane set in it. The gold letters on the glass said DR. AMALIA PIMLICO. As he reached for the knob, Johnny's hand was shaking, and for the twentieth time he told himself that there was nothing at all to be afraid of. He grasped the cold brass knob and twisted it. The door opened.

Johnny walked into a cheerful sunlit office decorated with a lovely cool green oriental rug and off-white walls.

Near the door stood a tall glass display case showing many pairs of eyeglasses, and an eye chart hung on one wall. A chair, like one found in a dentist's office, was on the right with all sorts of eye-testing equipment hanging over it on jointed metal arms. At the far end of the room, near the windows, stood an oak desk, and behind the desk sat Dr. Amalia Pimlico. She was a heavyset elderly woman in a white hospital uniform, and she looked very cheerful and pleasant. Her gray hair was pulled into a bun, and she wore steel-rimmed spectacles. In one hand she held a pen, and she seemed to be in the middle of writing something.

"Good afternoon, young man," said the doctor, smiling. "You must be John Dixon, and you're here to have your eyes examined. Am I correct?"

Johnny nodded. He was so jittery that he would have started stammering if he had tried to speak.

Dr. Pimlico's smile got broader. She motioned for Johnny to come closer. Awkwardly he shuffled forward. He noticed an odd collection of things lying on the doctor's desk: a wide roll of adhesive tape, a pair of scissors, a neatly folded white handkerchief, and a hypodermic syringe full of some clear fluid. Nervously Johnny glanced to his left. There was a doorway there, and it probably led to an inner office. Over the doorway hung a dark green curtain.

Dr. Pimlico cocked her head to one side. Her smile was still pleasant, but there was a hard glint in her eyes. Johnny was trembling all over by now, and when he opened his mouth to speak, he found that he couldn't. He closed his eyes, and in that instant, he heard the curtain slide back on its rings. Hands grabbed his shoulders from behind. He knew that he was a prisoner. He knew he was doomed.

CHAPTER FOURTEEN

The professor was enjoying himself, as he always did when he rummaged around in a used bookstore. He loved the smell of damp paper, and the tables loaded with old, battered, dog-eared books. As he browsed, he talked to himself, and sometimes he whistled bits of old tunes, like "Lilliburlero" and the "Londonderry Air." Now and then he would make remarks to the owner, a grumpy fat man who sat at the back of the shop playing solitaire on the counter.

"What time is it, Al?" the professor called as he leafed through a book. "I left my watch at home, and I have to pick up a young man who is visiting the eye doctor."

The owner shifted in his seat and peered at a clock that hung somewhere in the shadows at the back of the shop.

"It's 'bout quarter to three," he said wheezily. "That is, if the clock's right, which sometimes it's not."

"Thanks a lot," muttered the professor, and he grinned wryly. Whether the clock was right or not, he was going to browse for maybe ten minutes more. Putting the book down, he moved across the shop to another table. But just as he was reaching to pull another book out of the disorderly heap, he noticed something that interested him. Hanging on the wall above the table was an old faded tea towel. It was obviously a souvenir, because the design on it was a map of the London Underground, the English subway system. The professor had ridden on the Underground many times, and he loved the odd names that many of the stops had: Cockfosters, Hanger Lane, Shepherds Bush, and his favorite, Elephant and Castle. Whistling quietly, the professor examined the map. Suddenly he stopped whistling. Not far from the center of the map he had found two names, two subway stops that were fairly close together. One was *Sloane Square*, and the other was *Pimlico*. Sloane. Pimlico. Pimlico. Sloane.

The professor felt cold all over. The palms of his hands got sweaty, and his heart began to beat faster. Had he stumbled on to something important, or was this just a trick of his imagination? Pimlico was an odd name for a person to have, a very odd name indeed. The professor realized that he did not know very much about Evaristus Sloane's life. He knew that he had left New Hampshire when he was in his thirties, but he did not know where he had gone. Had he gone to London? Was that where he had picked up that English accent? And had he met . . . had he met . . .

"*Good God! His WIFE!*" roared the professor. As the startled shop owner watched, the professor flung down the book he was holding and made a dash for the door.

A few minutes later, the professor's car came to a screeching halt in front of the First National Bank building. The professor jumped out and raced into the bank, leaving the car door hanging open behind him. After pausing for a moment by the elevators, he ran to the stairs. Not many old men could have raced up five flights of stairs without stopping, but the professor did. On the way he elbowed people out of the way and yelled things like "I'll *kill* her, so help me, I will!" At last he reached the door of Dr. Pimlico's office, and he rattled the knob furiously. His heart sank. As he had guessed, the place was locked up tight. A small white card was taped to the frosted glass with this message neatly printed:

> Due to an illness in her family, Dr. Pimlico has been called away suddenly. She should return in about two weeks.

The professor stood clenching and unclenching his fists. His face was getting red, and he felt an uncontrollable rage welling up inside his chest. He wanted to seize this so-called "Dr. Pimlico" by the shoulders and shake her. She was long gone. For a moment the professor thought about smashing the glass and breaking into the office, but he realized that it would be useless. Besides, he'd better not hang around much longer—the bank guards were probably on their way up to the fifth floor to catch the crazy old man who was loose in the building. With an angry, frustrated sigh, the professor turned away. As he went clumping down the back stairs, it suddenly occurred to him that he understood one of the clues. Johnny had met the snuffbox ghost three times: twice the ghost had spoken, and each time it had said the same thing—*They took my eyes*! The professor had wondered who *they* were—he had always figured that Sloane worked by himself. *But he had help*, muttered the professor to himself. *The old bat had been with him, even then. It's a fine time for me to find out about that, now that she's taken Johnny! A fine time!*

By the time he got back to his car, the professor had begun to calm down a bit. He realized with a sinking heart that he would have to tell Gramma and Grampa what had happened. At least he wouldn't have to tell them the *whole* truth, he said to himself with a shudder. He wouldn't have to explain about the robot, and spell out the reasons why Evaristus Sloane wanted Johnny. But it was going to be difficult enough to tell them that Johnny had been kidnaped.

When he got to the Dixons' house, the professor discovered that they had already heard the bad news. Grampa came to the door with a tear-stained face and a note in his hand. It was a sheet of dime-store tablet paper with a message printed on it in big black capital letters.

YOUR GRANDSON IS WITH US. WE DO
NOT WANT A RANSOM, BUT WE NEED
YOUR COOPERATION. DO NOT TRY TO
STOP US WHEN WE PUT OUR PLAN
INTO ACTION. LATER, JOHN WILL BE
RETURNED TO YOU.

As the professor read the note, he found that his scrambled thoughts were beginning to straighten out. He already knew that Dr. Pimlico's nephew had entered the strikeout contest, but now he realized that the "nephew" had to be Sloane's robot. The old devil had rescued one of the robots from the house—but which one? The professor thought a bit, and he realized that it had to be the old one, the fifty-year-old baseball-pitching robot. The house on Mount Creed had burned down on the night of September 27th. Even if Sloane had stolen someone's eyes that very night, he wouldn't have had time to activate the new robot: it took forty days for the spell to be completed, and the strikeout contest was on October 15th, three days from now. *All right*, the professor told himself. *So they're going to use the robot, and they knew I'd figure out what they were up to. This note is really a warning to me, so I won't try to interfere with their wonderful plans. By heaven, I'd like to wring their necks!*

As the professor stood there on the Dixons' front porch,

his mind was racing. He clutched the note and made squinchy faces. Suddenly he snapped out of his trance and remembered where he was. Grampa was staring at him strangely.

"Rod?" asked Grampa. "What's the matter with you? You act like you was off on Cloud Nine."

The professor blinked and frowned. "I'm not on Cloud Nine," he snapped tartly. "I'm down in the flames of Hell, sticking pitchforks into two very nasty people. Look, Henry—I think I know who kidnaped Johnny, and I even have some vague idea of why they did it. But I don't want you to do anything. Don't tell the police, don't even tell the neighbors. If anyone asks about Johnny, tell them he's gone to see his father at that Air Force base in Virginia. We've got to move carefully, and if we do the wrong thing, Johnny might lose his life. Do you understand me?"

Grampa nodded sadly. "I guess so. But doncha think we oughta tell the police? I mean—"

"Absolutely not!" said the professor, shaking his head violently. "The police of this town would mess up a tic-tac-toe game if you put it into their hands. We've got to keep this whole business secret for a while. In the meantime, I will tell you that Fergie and I will be going to the strikeout contest on the fifteenth. You and Kate are welcome too, but you might be happier if you . . . By the way, where is Kate? Is she all right?"

Grampa jerked his thumb toward the back of the house. "She's in the downstairs bedroom, lyin' down. When this rotten note came, she darn near had a conniption fit; she cried an' took on somethin' awful! I think she'll be okay though—she's a pretty tough old cookie. But if you don't mind tellin' me, why the blue blazes are you an' Fergie goin' to the strikeout thing? An' what the heck does that have to do with Johnny gettin' kidnaped?"

The professor pursed his lips and scratched his ear. "I hate to be so secretive," he said with a sad smile, "but if I tried to explain this whole weird business to you, you would think I had gone off my rocker. I will say this: I think John will be safe until that stupid contest is over. But after, he's going to be in terribly great danger, and that is why we have to go find him and find him fast!" The professor paused. Then he smiled sympathetically and patted Grampa on the elbow. "Have faith in me, old friend," he said softly. "I've helped Johnny out of some bad scrapes in the past, and I'm sure I can save him again. But you have to do what I've told you. Will you?"

Again Grampa nodded. "Sure, Rod. I trust you." He held out his hand for the professor to shake. "Good luck!"

"Thanks. I will most certainly need it!" said the professor, as he shook Grampa's hand. "I'll talk to you later." And with that, he turned on his heel and marched back across the street. As he walked, his mind was churning out plans and strategies. He would have to call Fergie and tell him that he was going to the strikeout contest. Fergie didn't know it yet, but he *was* going, if the professor had to drag him there by the heels. Actually, Fergie probably wouldn't need much persuading—he loved excitement, and excitement there would be if the professor's clever plan worked. Now if only . . .

The professor paused in his front hall and struggled to make his feverish brain calm down. He was thinking of too many things at once, and he needed to be orderly and logical, if he could possibly manage it. Nervously he glanced around the dusty hallway and happened to notice the umbrella stand and the mysterious sword cane. Now *there* was something utterly, totally illogical: the ghost had led them to the cane, but what were they supposed to do with it? Were they supposed to use it to kill Evaristus Sloane? *If that's what he wants, he's out of luck*, said the professor to himself. He was a cantankerous person, but he did not believe in killing people, even when they had done horrible things. Besides, killing Sloane would not get Johnny back. However, cold steel could look pretty threatening, couldn't it? The professor went to the stand, pulled out the cane, and drew the blade half out of its sheath. With a loud *hrumph!* he slid the blade back and stuck the cane into the rack. Then he dashed into the house to make some phone calls.

CHAPTER FIFTEEN

Johnny lay still and stared at the sunlight that seeped through a crack in the rough wooden wall. Then he shifted a little, and the springs of the iron cot jangled under him. He groaned, but the sound was faint—a handkerchief had been stuffed into his mouth, and the lower part of his face was wrapped in a tight band of adhesive tape. His hands were flung above his head and fastened to the cot with two pairs of handcuffs. He was in a strange, dilapidated room. Long iron levers stuck up out of slits in the floor, and a faded calendar was tacked to the wall nearby. In the middle of the room stood a rickety oak table with an oil lamp and Thermos on top of it, and two cane-bottomed chairs. The door on the far side of the room opened, and two people stepped in: the eye doctor and the gaunt old man named Evaristus Sloane. After glancing scornfully at Johnny, the woman walked to the table, pulled out a chair, and sat down. With a sigh, Sloane followed her. When he was seated, he unscrewed the top of the Thermos and poured some steaming liquid into the cup-shaped lid. He sipped, and then gave the woman a nasty look. For a long time neither one of them said anything.

Finally Sloane spoke. "I don't care what you say, it *will* work. I know it will. I've learned a lot in fifty years, and I can control the wretched creature now."

The woman laughed harshly. "Let us hope that you do better than you did back then. As I recall, you lost the key, and the thing went hog-wild and killed three people before you found the key and got it under control again."

"Yes," put in Sloane bitterly. "And then people blamed the murders on me! They thought the robot was a madman who was living with me. So then I had to tear the creature apart and store it away and leave my lovely home and—"

"Yes, yes!" said the woman impatiently. "I know all about it! I was up there, I helped you make the robot—remember? And now you're going to use it again to win that silly contest. Wonderful! All I'm saying is this: I would have been happier if you had been able to rescue your *new* robot from the house before it burned down. It was almost finished, and you had laid spells on it. I have a hunch it would have been better than the old one."

"Well, what's done is done," said Sloane bitterly. "I was going to try to save both of them, but I knocked over the oil lamp on my way out. Besides, I knew I had to leave because that runty little man, that professor, was going to call the police. At any rate, my dear Amalia, we are stuck with my old robot. I never wanted to use it again after the things that it did, but it's back in action, and I'm sure it'll work better this time." Sloane paused and sipped from the cup. "And I'll tell you something," he went on, "this silly baseball contest is just the beginning. It's only a test run to show you that the robot can be controlled, that it can work wonders. Just think! We'll have a burglar who can pass through the steel doors of bank vaults and come back with gold and fistfuls of jewels and hundred dollar bills! We'll both be unbelievably rich!"

"So you say," the woman muttered. She pursed her lips and looked doubtful. "I am probably a fool to let myself be drawn into this plan with you, but—as you say—there may be great rewards. At any rate, if the robot fails again, you can always go to work and build a better one. It wouldn't take long, and as you know, we have the essential ingredient right here with us." She grinned unpleasantly, and glanced over her shoulder at Johnny.

Johnny closed his eyes and made a muffled groaning sound. He was sick with fear. It was bad enough knowing that they were going to kill him, but when he thought of the other things they might do, it was much, much worse. He was absolutely sure that they intended to get rid of him—they hadn't said so in so many words, but then

) 143 (

they didn't have to. When your kidnappers sat around and talked as if you weren't there, when they made no attempt to disguise themselves, you knew what was going to happen. *I wonder if it will hurt to die*, thought Johnny. Maybe they would give him a bigger dose of the stuff they had shot into his arm in the doctor's office. Then he would just go to sleep for ever and ever. But he didn't want that, he wanted to fight them. Frantically, Johnny tugged at the handcuffs. He lifted his head from the pillow and made mooing noises.

"I think we ought to give the boy something to drink," said Sloane. "He's probably out of his head with thirst."

"Aren't you the sympathetic one!" crooned the woman nastily. "But I suppose you're right—we wouldn't want him to die on us. Not yet, anyway." She turned again and grinned at Johnny. "Calm down, young man. If you thrash about you'll choke on that handkerchief, and then where'll you be?" Turning back to Sloane, she pointed at the Thermos. "Bring that over to the bed, Ev. I have some more tape in my purse, and we can do up his mouth again after we've given him a drink of tea and a bite to eat. And then I think we had better be on our way back to Duston Heights. You need to practice some more with that robot so that you can get him to do the right things at the ball park tomorrow night."

"If we leave him up here alone, do you think anyone will find him?" asked Sloane.

The woman sniffed. "I don't think there's much chance of that. An old railroad switchman's house on an abandoned railway in the White Mountains does not exactly draw hordes of gawking tourists. So stop your fretting, and we'll attend to our friend here."

The chair creaked as the woman got up. With her purse in her hand, she walked over to the bed and knelt down near Johnny's head. As she reached out to loosen the tape over his lips, her eyes met Johnny's, and his blood froze. Old Sloane was crazy—he knew that—but this woman was sane. Sane, but absolutely heartless. Johnny knew that she wouldn't mind causing him pain—she wouldn't mind killing him.

On the following night, a large crowd of people gathered at the athletic field in Duston Heights to watch Cliff Bullard as he went to bat against the best pitchers that Essex County had to offer. The banks of lights over the field were blazing, and there was a carnival atmosphere inside the small brick stadium—people were laughing and talking, and munching hot dogs, caramel corn, and peanuts. It was a chilly night, and the man who was selling hot coffee and hot cider under the stands was doing a lively business. In the front row on the first-base side sat Fergie and Professor Childermass. Gramma and Grampa had decided to stay home—they were too worried about Johnny to think about having fun. Fergie was looking all shiny and clean in his brown suede jacket and corduroy trousers. He spent a lot of time muttering to the professor, who kept nodding and pointing at various things. The professor was properly done up for the occasion: he was

wearing his blue woollen suit with the Knights of Colum-
bus pin in the lapel, and he had brought the sword cane
with him. Fergie wondered why he had brought the cane,
but then he was wondering a lot right now about the professor's great plan—it all seemed pretty screwy to him.

"Do you think it's gonna work, prof?" whispered
Fergie. "How's Higgy gonna get close enough to the
robot to do somethin' like that?"

The professor glowered. "You haven't been *listening*
to me, Byron!" he growled. And once more he explained
his plan: Father Higgins, the pastor of St. Michael's church
in Duston Heights, was going to be the umpire of the
strikeout contest. Since the robot was a cursed thing,
brought to life by evil magic, the professor thought that
a dose of holy water would stop it. Father Higgins would
be bringing a corked test tube with some of the blessed
water, and he was going to slop some on the baseball before giving it to the robot, when the creature came out
to pitch against Cliff Bullard.

"It's going to be sort of a spitball in reverse," said the
professor with a grim chuckle. "I haven't got the faintest
idea of what will happen when that aluminum monster
touches the holy water. Maybe he'll run away shrieking,
or maybe his pitching arm will rust all to pieces and fall
off. What I'm hoping for is that people will get to see
what kind of a creature he really is. At any rate, I think
the holy water will put an end to the robot's pitching
career, and then we can turn our attention to Sloane and
his dear sweet wifey. If the robot is stopped, I think that

they'll get scared and run. I borrowed Higgy's Olds-mobile, and I'll follow them to wherever they're holding Johnny. And then . . . Well, we shall see what we shall see."

Fergie glanced uncertainly at the professor. "Have you got a gun with you, prof?"

The professor gave Fergie a scornful look. "You know that I detest firearms, Byron," he said. "That is why I have brought this sword cane along. I can use it to threaten the two of them, and if I have to, I can defend myself. After all, I was the fencing champion of my regiment during World War One."

Fergie glanced at the professor doubtfully. He was about to say something when the professor poked him hard in the arm.

"Look! Here comes Higgy!" whispered the professor excitedly. "Now we'll see what's what!"

Fergie looked up and saw Father Higgins walking to-ward them across the baseball diamond. He was wearing his black clerical outfit with the stiff Roman collar and an umpire's padded chest protector. Father Higgins was over six feet tall, and he had a squarish jowly face. He was frowning, but this did not mean anything—Father Higgins often frowned, even when he was feeling fine. When he saw Fergie, the priest smiled and waved. Fergie had once played on a softball team that the priest had coached, and they were old friends.

"Hi, Byron!" boomed the priest. "How goes it?" He reached into the stands and shook Fergie's hand. Then he turned to the professor, and the grim look returned to his face. "I'm afraid we've got problems, Rod," he said softly. "Can I have a word with you in private?"

The professor stared blankly. What could have happened? Without a word he got up and swung himself over the low brick wall that separated the field from the stands. Fergie watched as the two men walked a short way out into right field and stood there on the grass, talking. After a few minutes, Father Higgins turned away and trotted across the field toward home plate, where Cliff Bullard was standing with a bat in his hands. The professor returned to his seat, and Fergie saw that he was very pale. The corner of his mouth was twitching, and his hand shook as he picked up the cane.

"What's wrong?" asked Fergie breathlessly. "What'd Higgy say?"

"He said a great deal," the professor muttered through his teeth. "But the gist of it is this: He's lost the tube with the holy water in it."

Fergie's mouth dropped open. "Oh, my gosh, no! How'd *that* happen?"

"He doesn't know. He put the tube in a satchel that held some of his umpiring equipment, and he left the satchel in the locker room under the stands for a few minutes. When he went back to get it, the satchel was still there, but the tube was gone!" The professor paused. He banged the butt of his cane on the concrete floor. "*Blast!*" he exclaimed angrily. "It seems that some people are a lot more clever than we give them credit for! That old bat knows I'm on to her, and she probably guessed that we'd try something cute tonight. I'm afraid we're on our own now!"

Fergie's heart sank. "Prof?" he asked in an anxious whisper. "What're we gonna do now?"

"I don't know," the professor answered quietly. "If I think of something, I'll let you know."

CHAPTER SIXTEEN

~∞~

RITTY CHITTY BOOM!
RITTY CHITTY BOOM!
RITTY CHITTY, RITTY CHITTY
ROT BAM BOOM!

With a riffle and rattle of snare drums, the Duston Heights High School marching band paraded out onto the field. Then, as everyone stood, they played "The Star-Spangled Banner." The drumming resumed, and they trotted off the field double-time. The preliminaries were over. Now the fun would begin.

First came a home-run hitting exhibition. A pitcher who traveled with Cliff Bullard went out to the mound and served up batting-practice pitches. Bullard hit them all over the place. One shot disappeared over the top of the center-field scoreboard, 450 feet away from home plate. Others went rocketing over the roof of the grandstand, and still others landed in the center-field bleachers, where kids chased them down and proudly carried them off as souvenirs. Finally it was time for the strikeout contest. As photographers popped their flashbulbs, Bullard posed at home plate and a voice on the public address system explained the rules: There would be ten pitchers in the contest, and each pitcher would get one try. Every try would be like a regular time at bat during a baseball game: if Bullard hit the ball or drew a walk, he won. If the pitcher struck him out, he won ten thousand dollars. Nobody really thought that any of the pitchers on the list could whiff the mighty Bullard, but it would be fun to see if somebody came close.

"It'd almost be worth it to see that wretched robot strike him out," muttered the professor as the first pitcher began his warm-up tosses. "I'd love to see the look on that big mug's face when the ball came sizzling in at one hundred and ten miles an hour!"

"Well, we're probably gonna get to see it happen," said Fergie gloomily. "Unless, of course, you've had any bright ideas, prof. Have you?"

"Not one," said the professor. He reached into his jacket pocket and took out a folded sheet of yellow paper. Sheets like this one had been handed out to everyone at the entrance to the stadium—they listed the pitchers in the order in which they would appear. Quickly the professor ran his finger down the row of names: Charles Hebden,

Al McGee, Jack Humphrey, Spencer Talus . . .

The professor's finger stopped on the name *Spencer Talus*. "*Ah-hah!*" he said, and he gave Fergie a nudge in the ribs. "This fourth name on the list has got to be the robot! Talus is the name of the iron man in a fairy-tale poem by an old writer named Edmund Spenser. My, my! Aren't they the clever ones! So he's going to be fourth on the list—we won't have to wait long, it seems!"

"Have you seen those two creeps?" Fergie asked. "Sloane and his wife. I mean, are they here?"

The professor nodded. "Oh, they're here all right! They're sitting across the way, in box seats behind the third-base line. And I'm sure they're chortling and cackling about the money they're going to make, and the evil rotten things they're going to do later." The professor thought about Johnny, and his face grew hard. "By heaven," he said, in a low voice, "it's a good thing I hate guns! I'd be tempted to take a pot shot at them from where I'm sitting. By the way, I think I will have a closer look at them, just to make myself feel bad."

He reached in under his seat and came up with a battered leather case. From it he took an old-fashioned pair of field glasses. Twiddling the little wheel, he scanned the crowd on the other side of the stadium, and finally focused in on the evil pair: Sloane was wearing dark glasses and a droopy white fake mustache; his wife was in a maroon tailored suit and pillbox hat. Her purse was balanced on her knees, and she clutched it tight with both hands.

"Ah, there they are, the Gruesome Twosome!" muttered the professor. "If you wanted to lose weight, all you'd have to do would be to look at them, and it'd kill your appetite for days! By the way, I'll bet the old hag has the Key of Arbaces in that purse she's holding. That's how they control the—"

The professor's little monologue was cut off by a loud burst of applause. Cliff Bullard had stepped into the batter's box. Father Higgins and the catcher took their places behind the batter. The pitcher went into his windup, and the ball came whizzing in. *Wok!* Bullard swung, and the ball went sailing in a long majestic arc into the left-field stands. The first pitcher had failed, and now the second came on. He had a pretty good curveball, but he had trouble getting it in there for strikes. The count ran to three balls and two strikes, and then the pitcher made a mistake: a fastball right across the middle of the plate. Bullard sent it rattling off the right-field fence. Then Jack Humphrey had his try: his specialty was a knuckleball, but it wasn't a very good one, and Bullard golfed Mr. Humphrey's third pitch high into the air. The ball sailed up over the roof of the left-field stands and disappeared into the night.

The crowd applauded. Bullard grinned and tipped his hat to the stands, and the people roared in response. It was really a grand night for Bullard, at least it had been so far. As the cheering continued Bullard took a brief time out. He walked to the home-team dugout, had a glass of water, and mopped his face with a towel. Then he slowly returned to the plate. A figure stepped out of the visitors' dugout across the way. It was a tall man with a big mop of blond hair and staring blue eyes. He walked stiffly, and as he advanced an odd hush fell over the crowd. Even Bullard paused and watched silently—he seemed to sense that this was no ordinary person coming to challenge him. The name of Spencer Talus was announced over the P.A. system, and a polite ripple of applause greeted him. Father Higgins walked out to the mound to give Talus the baseball and explain a few things to him. The big blond man nodded as the priest spoke, and he held his hand out awkwardly to take the ball. But instead of handing the ball to the pitcher, Father Higgins did an odd thing: He raised his right hand and made the sign of the cross in the air. The robot staggered back a couple of paces, but then it stopped. Angrily it lurched forward and grabbed the ball from the priest. A murmur ran through the crowd as people realized that something peculiar was going on. For a few seconds more, the priest and the robot faced each other. Then Father Higgins turned away and started walking slowly back to home plate.

"Nice try, Higgy!" said the professor with a sour grimace. He gripped the handle of his cane tightly and leaned forward. Was this it, then? Were they going to have to stand by and watch while that hunk of junk struck Cliff Bullard out? Would they have to sit tight and hope that Sloane and his creepy wife would let Johnny go unharmed? The professor felt helpless anger rising inside him. What could he possibly do?

The robot raised its hands to belt level—apparently it

was going to pitch from the stretch and not use a windup. Back went the arm, and around it came. A loud *thock!* sounded as the ball hit the catcher's mitt, and Bullard stood staring in disbelief with the bat on his shoulder.

"STEEEErike ONE!" boomed Father Higgins, and his right hand shot up.

An excited buzzing began in the crowd, and then it died away as the catcher flipped the ball back to the robot. Bullard pounded the plate and looked grim. He took little practice swings and yelled something out to the tall menacing figure on the mound. Once again, the robot began its pitching motion. The arm was a blur as it swept around, and this time Bullard swung mightily. But the ball was in the mitt before he had finished his swing.

"STEEEErike TWO!" bellowed the priest, and the crowd roared. This was great! It was really going to happen! A local boy was going to strike out the great Cliff Bullard of the New York Yankees! The cheering, stomping, and whistling went on for a long time, and Father Higgins had to raise his arms to get the people to quiet down. Finally the crowd hushed, and the robot toed the pitching rubber. Bullard looked pale and shaken, but he stepped into the batter's box again and raised his bat. . . .

"YOU DIRTY ROTTEN FRAUD!" screeched the professor, and he sprang to his feet. As the people around him watched in horror, the old man unsheathed the springy glittering sword, flourished it over his head, and vaulted up onto the brick wall in front of his seat. Then he leaped onto the field and went galloping madly toward the pitcher's mound. With heavy, lumbering steps the robot moved forward to meet him, and the baseball dropped from its hand. The professor advanced slowly. With the sword held out in front of him, he went into a dueler's stance. One whack of the robot's arm could crush his skull—the professor knew that.

"*Now then, come on, sir!*" yelled the professor tauntingly. "*We must have a drop or two of this malapert blood from you!*"

The robot swung, and the professor ducked. He felt the rush of the powerful arm as it passed over his head. The professor dashed around behind the robot. Frantically he searched for the shadowy hole in the back of its neck . . . was it there? Ah, yes, it was! Before the creature could turn round to face him, the professor raised the sword and plunged the tip of it into the slit. A shudder ran through the robot's body. It staggered drunkenly forward. With loud curses and yells, the professor plunged the sword's tip into the hole again and again and again. But the robot did not collapse. It was turning round to face him, and the professor felt sick with fear. Had he merely angered the creature? Was that all he had done? The professor heard angry yelling, and he realized that people were running toward him. At first everyone had been too shocked to move, but now at last two policemen had leaped onto the field, pistols drawn. They pounded toward him shouting "*Stop!*" and "*You're under arrest!*" And then something happened. . . .

As everyone watched, the air around the robot shimmered. It did not look like a tall, blue-eyed man anymore —it was a grotesque, shiny metal statue with eerie glass eyes. Awkwardly the thing flung its right arm up. With a loud snapping sound, the arm fell off and hit the ground with a thud. The robot opened its jaw wide to let out a hideous, unearthly screech. The professor dropped his sword and covered his ears—the noise was unbearable. He closed his eyes tight, and when he opened them a second later, the robot was lying motionless on the grass.

More and more people poured onto the field, and soon there was a ring of astonished faces around the professor and the dead robot. The professor felt extremely tired. Sweat was pouring down his face and he was gasping for breath. He stared silently at the two policemen, and they looked back in utter dumbfounded amazement. Then there was a loud commotion as somebody came shoving through the crowd. It was Sloane's wife, and she was hopping mad. Her face was twisted into a red mask of rage, and she lunged at the professor with her pocketbook raised high over her head.

"You meddling old fool!" she screeched. *"You filthy old man! What have you done? He's dead! You killed him!"*

Two men grabbed Mrs. Sloane, and they held her while she struggled. Wearily the professor turned to her. He was about to say that there was no law against killing robots, but then a thought occurred to him. "Where . . .

where's Sloane?" he asked, in a dazed, dreamy voice.

"*I told you!*" she yelped. "*He's dead! His heart couldn't stand it! I'd like to break your filthy neck!*"

The professor scowled at the woman contemptuously. He turned to the policemen. "Gentlemen," he said quietly, "you had better take this harpy away and lock her up. She and her late husband kidnaped Johnny Dixon a few days ago, and they have been holding him prisoner God knows where. I will come down to the police station and make formal charges against her, and hopefully we can find out where Johnny is and rescue him. If you don't mind, I believe I left my binoculars under my seat, and I'd better go fetch them. I'll see you in a few minutes."

Stooping, the professor picked up the sword. Fergie was at his side now—he had come running out with everyone else. The professor smiled at Fergie and patted his arm, and then the two of them started back across the field. The crowd parted to let them pass, and everyone started to cheer. The professor raised his hand to wave, but then he dropped it. He felt triumphant, but he also felt unbelievably tired, and he began to think about how nice it would be to be home in bed, sound asleep.

CHAPTER SEVENTEEN

Needless to say, there was a lot of talk about the strange thing that had happened at the Duston Heights athletic field on the night of the big strikeout contest. Everybody in the city had an opinion of some kind, and you couldn't find two people who had the same version of what had happened. Some said that it was a supernatural event, that it couldn't be explained any other way; others claimed that it was a cheap sleight-of-hand trick, an illusion that had been performed with mirrors. Many people raved that they had known all along that the tall blond pitcher was really a robot and that the poor lighting at the stadium had helped to fool people; and a few claimed that the robot really *had* been human, and that the professor had murdered Mr. Talus for some obscure reason. Cliff Bullard was interviewed the day after the contest, and he was hopping mad. He said the whole thing was a rotten swindle arranged by somebody—he didn't want to say who. He added that he would sue the dirty so-and-so who had embarrassed him as soon as he saw his lawyer back in New York City.

As for the robot, it was carted away to the city dump—after the professor had pulled out its eyes and smashed them into powder with the jack handle that he kept in his car. A hearse was called to the stadium to carry away the body of an elderly man who had died of a heart attack in his seat, and Dr. Amalia Pimlico was taken to the police station for questioning. Kidnaping is a federal offense, so two F.B.I. agents were called in, and they grilled Dr. Pimlico for some time. At first she was stubborn, but finally she broke down and told the police everything they wanted to know. A helicopter was sent to the abandoned switchman's house in the White Mountains, and Johnny was flown immediately to a local hospital. He was dehydrated because he hadn't had any water for a long time, but he recovered quickly. After two days he was allowed to go home.

While Johnny was recovering, the professor did some snooping. He drove up to Emmett Oglesby's gas station in Stark Corners and poked around and pried up floorboards until he found what he wanted: a journal that Sloane had kept. In it—among other things—was a day-by-day account of the life the old man had led since he came back to Stark Corners. Some letters were stuffed into the journal, and these were helpful too—at least, the professor thought they were.

Finally, when Johnny was feeling better, Professor Coote invited everybody up to a party at his cottage on Lake Winnepesaukee. Gramma and Grampa, Fergie, the professor, and Johnny all went, and the party was a lot of fun: there was plenty to eat and drink, and Professor Coote took everyone for a moonlight cruise on the *Mount Washington*, a large old-fashioned excursion boat. Later, everyone was sitting around stuffed and happy on the porch of the cottage, and the two professors started to talk about Evaristus Sloane and his magic robot.

"So, Roderick," said Professor Coote as he sipped his brandy, "you really didn't know there was writing on the blade of that silly sword! I think that's extremely funny— I mean, you *are* a scholar and everything!"

"Har de har har!" said the professor grumpily. "It's a big fat joke, isn't it? All right, I'll admit it—I was fooled. I know several languages, but Arabic isn't one of them. I thought all those squirls and squiggles were just a decorative pattern. Humph! And so it seems that the ghost of the man whose eyes were stolen wanted vengeance, and he gave us a weapon to use. But why on earth didn't he just *say* what he wanted us to do with the sword?"

Professor Coote smiled smugly. "Roderick, I'm ashamed of you!" he said. "You know as much about folklore as I do, and you should be aware that ghosts are very often tongue-tied. They appear and mumble something and frighten the dickens out of us. Then they leave us to try and figure out what it is they want us to do. In the end, of course, you didn't figure out what the sword was for—you just survived by pure dumb luck!"

The professor shrugged. "Well, luck or not, it was a darned good thing I brought the cane with me to the stadium the other night!"

"It certainly is!" put in Professor Coote emphatically. "If you had sprayed that robot with machine gun fire, he would just have brushed the bullets away like flies. If you had tried to jam an ordinary sword's point into that keyhole, you would just have wound up with a broken sword. It takes magic to fight magic! By the way, Roderick, would you care to read the inscription to our friends here? It might interest them."

Professor Childermass reached into the pocket of his suit coat and took out a white card. On it was written Professor Coote's translation of the writing on the blade of the magic sword:

This is the Sword of Righteousness, dipped thrice in the waters of the River Jordan at midnight, during the moon's eclipse. Wield it against the servant of the Evil One and God will prevail.

The professor read these words aloud in a solemn voice, and then he flipped the card out onto the middle of the porch rug. "How about that?" he sighed. "I wonder who owned that sword originally—some Muslim wizard, maybe? Ah, well, it worked for us in our time of need, and that is what counts!"

There was silence for a while. In the distance, a motor-boat's sleepy drone could be heard. Then Johnny spoke up.

"Why did old Sloane want to use my eyes in his robot?" he asked plaintively. "I know he wanted to get even with Grampa, but . . . well, wouldn't a robot with nearsighted eyes be kind of useless?"

The professor looked pained. The whole business of Sloane and his evil plans really disgusted him, and he didn't like to talk about it. However, he felt that Johnny had a right to an answer. "In the first place," he began as he lit a cigarette, "I think we will all agree that Sloane was as nutty as a fruitcake. According to his journal, he had gotten it into his head that his robot really *ought* to have nearsighted eyes! And why, you will ask? Well, as far as I can figure out from the letters and newspaper clippings that I found in Sloane's journal, his original robot was not a huge success—it got loose and ran around killing people. Sloane decided that a robot with nearsighted eyes would be easier to control: he would equip it with glasses, but the glasses could be taken away if the robot started acting rambunctious. Or, if worse came to worst, Sloane could knock the glasses off with a pole or shatter them with a BB from an air rifle. Then the silly robot would stagger around and crash into trees until it collapsed, or until Sloane caught up with it and used the magic key to shut it off. But—"

"What happened to the key, anyway?" asked Fergie, interrupting. "Does old Mrs. Uglypuss still have it?"

The professor smiled smugly. "No, she most certainly does not! When she was put into her jail cell, her purse was taken away from her, and I managed to get my fat fist into it when no one was looking. I swiped the key and pitched it into the middle of Round Pond."

After a brief pause, Professor Coote spoke up. "You know, Roderick," he said, "the strangest part of this whole weird business is how that spectacle case with the glass eyes in it came to be left in a bush for you to find. Sloane must have hidden it away somewhere in or near the house, and maybe you're right in thinking that a robber found the case and then threw it away. But still, I keep wondering if some evil power meant for you to find those eyes. Doesn't it seem possible to you?"

The professor puffed on his cigarette and looked thoughtful. "Ye-es," he said slowly, "it does seem possible. And if I ever meet the evil power in a back alley, I will give it a fat lip and a couple of black eyes. Think of all the trouble those wretched glass eyes caused! It's incredible, isn't it?"

Silence again. Rockers creaked, and Grampa Dixon puffed quietly on his pipe. In a corner of the screened porch, a card table stood. On it was a bowl of pinkish punch, some paper cups, and a candle in a fancy china holder. As Johnny watched, the candle's flame flickered in the chilly night breeze. His life had been like that, a flickering flame in the dark, and if it hadn't been for the courage of his friends . . .

Suddenly Fergie spoke up. "Hey, prof! What're they gonna do to old Mrs. Pimlico, or whatever her name is?"

The professor sighed and blew out a stream of cigarette smoke. "She's going to stand trial on a kidnaping charge," he said calmly. "Johnny will have to testify, and I'm sure it'll be a disagreeable experience, but I will not be happy until that old bat is behind bars permanently—or at least, for twenty years. For the record, her real name is Amalia Sloane. She married Evaristus Sloane way back in the old days, when they were both young, and if those closemouthed people up in Stark Corners had told me about her in the first place, we might have been spared a good deal of trouble. I mean, we might have been on the lookout for her, instead of being taken by surprise the way we were."

"By the way, Roderick," Professor Coote asked, "did Sloane's wife stay with him during the time when he was away from Stark Corners?"

The professor shook his head. "No," he said, "she did not. As you know, he had to flee from the town because of the murderous deeds of his robot. At that time, he went to England, and she went somewhere else. But they stayed in contact by writing letters to each other, and over the long years Sloane dreamed up this idea of making a *better* robot, one that would loot bank vaults and make them both rich. Old Amalia was skeptical about this, but she was also greedy, so when they both wound up back in the United States again, she decided to throw in with him. As it happened, she had become an optometrist, and she decided to use her profession to find a victim for him. By a coincidence, she happened to set up her office here in Duston Heights. It was a coincidence that almost proved fatal to poor John here."

"She's a bad one, ain't she?" put in Grampa. "How can anybody be that rotten?"

"Oh, it's easy for some people," said the professor with a sour smile. "She has a heart like a brass door knocker. And now, for heaven's sake, let's talk about something else!" With that he pulled himself up out of his chair and went to get a cup of punch. As he was sipping, Professor Coote started to chuckle.

"Well?" snapped the professor, turning round and glaring at him. "What is it that's so incredibly funny? Eh?"

"Oh, not much, Roderick," said his friend, still laughing. "But have you heard what Cliff Bullard thinks about this whole affair? He remembered that you were the one who heckled him down in Fenway Park earlier this year, and so he thinks the whole thing with the robot was an elaborate practical joke that you dreamed up just to make him look foolish. He won't let anyone say in print that he suspects you, but the boys down at the *Gazette* office say that is what he really thinks."

"Cliff Bullard hasn't had a thought since he was in diapers," snapped the professor. "By the way, Charley, I have two tickets for a Yankees-Red Sox game down at Fenway in May. Would you care to go with me?"

"It depends on where the seats are," his friend shot back. "If we're close enough to the field for Bullard to recognize you, I wouldn't be there for all the money in the world."

Everybody laughed, and the professor's face got red. "I'll wear a fake beard and a stocking cap," he growled sarcastically.

"Will you promise not to shout and scream insults?" asked Professor Coote in a taunting voice.

"I won't promise in writing," the professor said, and the laughter got louder. It was a good sound, and Johnny was glad to join in.

JOHN BELLAIRS

is the critically acclaimed, best-selling author of many gothic novels, including *The House with a Clock in Its Walls; The Figure in the Shadows: The Letter, the Witch and the Ring; The Curse of the Blue Figurine; The Mummy, the Will, and the Crypt; The Dark Secret of Weatherend; The Spell of The Sorcerer's Skull;* and his latest tale, *The Eyes of the Killer Robot.* Mr. Bellairs has also written a number of adult books, among them *The Face in the Frost.*

A resident of Haverhill, Massachusetts, Mr. Bellairs is currently at work on another suspense thriller.

Enter the exciting wilderness with

JIM KJELGAARD

In these adventure stories, Jim Kjelgaard shows us the special world of animals, the wilderness, and the bonds between men and dogs. *Irish Red* and *Outlaw Red* are stories about two champion Irish setters. *Snow Dog* shows what happens when a half-wild dog crosses paths with a trapper. The cougar-hunting *Lion Hound* and the greyhound story *Desert Dog* take place in the Southwest. And, *Stormy* is an extraordinary story of a boy and his devoted dog. You'll want to read all of them.